ALLEN COUN
3 1833 02781 795 3
S0-BWY-654

SPECIAL MESSAGE TO READERS

This book is published under the auspices of

THE ULVERSCROFT FOUNDATION

(registered charity No. 264873 UK)

Established in 1972 to provide funds for research, diagnosis and treatment of eye diseases. Examples of contributions made are: —

A new Children's Assessment Unit at Moorfield's Hospital, London.

•

Twin operating theatres at the Western Ophthalmic Hospital, London.

•

A Chair of Ophthalmology at the University of Leicester.

•

The establishment of a Royal Australian College of Ophthalmologists "Fellowship".

You can help further the work of the Foundation by making a donation or leaving a legacy. Every contribution, no matter how small, is received with gratitude. Please write for details to:

THE ULVERSCROFT FOUNDATION,
The Green, Bradgate Road, Anstey,
Leicester LE7 7FU, England.
Telephone: (0116) 236 4325

In Australia write to:
THE ULVERSCROFT FOUNDATION,
c/o The Royal Australian College of Ophthalmologists,
27, Commonwealth Street, Sydney,
N.S.W. 2010.

ALL FOR JOLIE

Leonie was devastated when her best friend, Jolie, was killed in a car accident; they had always been more like sisters than friends. Whilst out for a drink with a business acquaintance one evening, Leonie met the man she thought was responsible for the accident — the driver of the car, Scott Andrews. She felt great anger towards Scott and decided to seek revenge for Jolie's death — but it was disturbing to find him so attractive.

Books by Eileen Knowles
in the Linford Romance Library:

THE ASTOR INHERITANCE
MISTRESS AT THE HALL

EILEEN KNOWLES

ALL FOR JOLIE

Complete and Unabridged

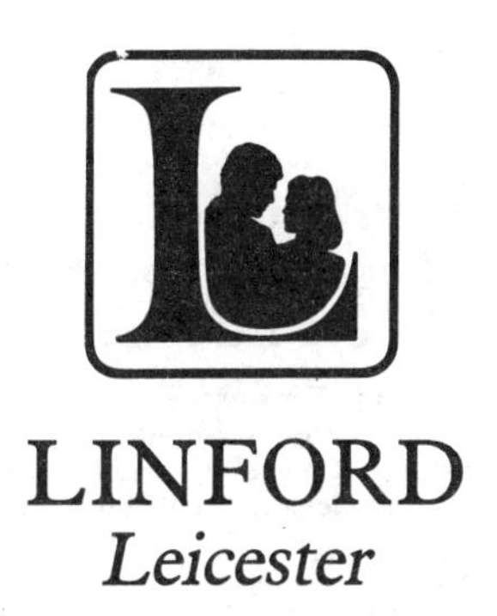

LINFORD
Leicester

First Linford Edition
published 1998

British Library CIP Data

Knowles, Eileen
All for Jolie.—Large print ed.—
Linford romance library
1. Love stories
2. Large type books
I. Title
823.9′14 [F]

ISBN 0–7089–5302–6

Published by
F. A. Thorpe (Publishing) Ltd.
Anstey, Leicestershire

Set by Words & Graphics Ltd.
Anstey, Leicestershire
Printed and bound in Great Britain by
T. J. International Ltd., Padstow, Cornwall

This book is printed on acid-free paper

1

HE was still alive! How was it possible? Leonie simply couldn't credit what she was reading. Scott Andrews had perished in the carnage on the motorway along with Jolene hadn't he? Sadness and remorse at the loss of someone as vivacious as her friend still brought tears to her eyes. Poor Jolene, she had obviously been misled again, only this time with tragic result! Leonie flopped back in her executive leather chair and breathed in deeply, her lips compressed with barely contained anger.

She was a slim, rather serious young woman with burnished auburn hair and eyes the colour of ripe hazelnuts. Her hair cascaded down her back in loose, unruly curls, as often as not casually held in a ribbon as a means of containing it. Many people thought it was her most pleasing feature, but to Leonie it was a constant trial. Wisps broke free and she pushed them back off her face with a familiar, yet unconscious action, as she turned her gaze to the photograph residing on the corner of her desk. The picture of a young girl — an attractive, happy, vibrant teenager grinned mockingly back.

Leonie threw the paper into her in-tray with disgust. Then, blinking away tears at the thought of Jolie's unfortunate end, vowed that she would exact revenge from the culprit. That miscreant in her eyes was none other than Scott Andrews — the man in the newspaper article — the man who until now she had thought to be dead — the man at the wheel of the car in which her friend died. Yes, it was his fault that Jolie was dead, and Leonie was now all alone in the world.

She had intended sending his family her condolences, but somehow, what with all the upset she hadn't done so. Now to learn that he was very much alive, and apparently fit and well incensed her. She dabbed her eyes with a tissue and recovered the paper to make certain of the facts, re-reading the part of the paragraph on the front page that had caught her eye. '*Scott Andrews of Andrews Electronics generously donated a computer . . .* ' She wished there had been a photograph of this *charitable benefactor*!

She tried to settle to work, but found it well nigh impossible, her mind kept wandering back to the tragedy, and what she could do to with the latest piece of information. Fortunately, being the boss had its privileges, there was no-one to complain that she wasn't pulling her weight. The secretarial agency that she had started with her redundancy money was progressing nicely.

She prided herself though on being totally committed to providing a quick, accurate and professional service second to none. At first the response had proved slightly disappointing, but then a friend of Jolie's was kind enough to recommend her to his friends, and soon the business began to grow. It wasn't long before she found the need to employ others, and so her army of helpers grew. Now she had several women to call on a part-time, as and when basis, which suited everyone. They were mainly housewives who had previously been typists or secretaries, and they fitted in the work around family commitments. Her one full-time member of staff was Tina who looked after the front office.

On the whole Leonie was well satisfied with her lifestyle. Her work meant everything to her. She felt justifiably proud of what she had attained, and she wasn't yet twenty-three. The only obstacle to her enjoyment was the death of Jolie. Despite their very different personalities they had become firm friends in the foster home where they were brought up. Leonie the serious, studious girl and Jolie the happy-go-lucky one. They had complemented each other in their different ways, both grateful for the other's companionship.

Leonie recalled Jolie's last phone call, the night before she died. She had been wildly excited about the latest boy friend she had acquired. She was quite ecstatic, but that was nothing unusual for her. Jolie always made everything and everyone sound wonderful and exciting, and always eager to participate in anything new. Her zest for travel and adventure had been her downfall. Only Jolie would be foolish enough to miss the train and then compound her irresponsibility by hitching a lift.

Leonie hadn't wanted her to go on the trip to Scotland in the first place, especially as the weather forecast had been poor. She didn't know why she had been apprehensive about the holiday, since Jolie was meeting up with a group of friends, and it wasn't the first time she had been skiing. It was a sport she thoroughly enjoyed — or so she said, although Leonie expressed the opinion that it was the après ski which appealed more. For some reason Leonie had felt troubled about the holiday from the start, but Jolie had laughed at her fears and gone anyway. If Leonie had known at the time about her accepting a lift from a stranger she would have been horrified, despite her friend's assurance that her knight errant was an absolute dream.

The intercom on her desk buzzed, its jarring tone startling Leonie back to reality.

"Your ten o'clock appointment is here," Tina reported. "Shall I send him up?"

"Yes, please do." Leonie quickly surveyed her diary to see who she was expecting, it had gone clean out of her head. She caught the terseness in Tina's tone intimating that she wasn't pleased to see the client, and now realised why. Censuring herself for too much wool gathering, Leonie went to the door to greet the visitor, feeling more than a little wary.

"Good morning, Simon. What can I do for you?" she asked offering him a chair. She went back to her own behind the desk, feeling happier to have its substantial barrier between them. Simon Dean made her nervous, but she couldn't afford to offend him. He was a local entrepreneur and one of Jolie's many acquaintances. Leonie had lost contact with most of Jolie's friends since the funeral, but Simon had kept in touch and put much business her way in the past few weeks. He had many contacts locally and seemed willing to recommend 'Girl Friday' so she tried to disregard his irritating ways.

Slowly Leonie was learning the skills necessary to be competitive and build a viable business, but still found some clients more intimidating than others. Simon Dean was one such individual, and she felt his eyes tauntingly undressing her. She had never met anyone who could embarrass her like he did. Even without speaking his manner was suggestive and crude. She could feel the colour rising in her cheeks, and surreptitiously clasped her hands tightly together out of sight under the desk in an effort to remain calm.

"Now there's an offer and no mistake!" He grinned lewdly. He enjoyed making her squirm — he always had, but she tried hard not to show how uncomfortable she felt in his presence. When Jolie had been alive it had been easier to ignore his ribald remarks, but now she found them in extremely poor taste. However business was business so one had to accept the odd unpleasantness, and fortunately most of her clients were not like him.

"Well, Simon. I know you are a busy man so I won't delay you longer than necessary by offering you coffee. How can 'Girl Friday' be of assistance?"

"I wouldn't mind some coffee," he replied suavely crossing his legs and lolling back as if he had all the time in the world. I'm never in a hurry to leave your establishment."

Leonie wished she hadn't mentioned coffee she might have known he would say he'd like some. She made a mental note for future reference not to repeat the mistake. She could have made it herself, she had all the facilities in the next room, but instead she rang down for Tina to bring a cup up for her guest. She had no wish for him to invade the privacy of her flat, and no doubt he would have followed her through to the kitchenette.

Simon Dean made small talk and waited until Tina had been and gone before at last getting round to discussing his latest requirements.

"My secretary has been whisked into hospital. I don't know how long she will be away and I need someone to take over, pronto. Obviously I immediately thought of you. I don't suppose you would consider standing in yourself? I'll gladly pay whatever you charge for *your* personal service. Jolie told me that you were the best in the business."

"Sorry," Leonie said quickly. "I'm fully booked. I'll be working most nights as it is. There's a 'flu epidemic going round Chellow. The phone has hardly stopped ringing all morning." It wasn't strictly true but she didn't want him getting any ideas about her having time spare to socialise. Every time they met he asked her out and so far she had managed to diplomatically avoid accepting.

"Since you need someone urgently I can recommend Jane. She's extremely capable and has no children, so hours aren't a problem. She should suit you perfectly. Shall I contact her to see if she's free?"

Simon pulled a face. "I suppose it's what I expected you to say. I hope she's pretty though. I don't want any old tartar. I don't mind if her shorthand isn't up to scratch, as long as she's young and nubile."

"Jane is attractive, but that is not why I employ her. She happens to be good at her job," Leonie said crisply, irritated by his patronising manner. She knew Jane would stand for no nonsense from him though, and could handle the likes of Simon Dean better than she could herself.

"OK." He gave a wily grin. "I was about to ask if you'd care to join me for a drink one evening. Surely you must have some time you can call your own?"

Leonie sighed. "That is most kind, Simon. I do appreciate it. It's ages since I had a night off, but I'm so busy. Maybe another time."

"That's what you always say. Come on, I won't take no for answer. You need a break. You're looking harassed — still missing Jolie? I'll pick you up at seven thirty, OK? It'll do you good to get out for an hour or so. Blow the paperwork. After all, all work, etc., etc. You know it's what Jolie would say."

What could she do but accept graciously.

* * *

"What did he want?" Tina asked, her eyebrows rose disparagingly as the door closed behind their visitor.

"Besides a secretary you mean?"

"Has he really got you to go out with him?"

"I can't afford to upset him for goodness sake. You know that. And besides he's only taking me for a drink, it shouldn't be too onerous."

Tina sniffed. "He's too smarmy for my liking. Got a finger in too many pies."

"He also helps pay your wages don't forget," Leonie reminded her, irritated by Tina's comments, even though privately they mirrored her own thoughts.

* * *

Leonie thought about what Tina had said as she got ready later that evening. Maybe Simon could help in her desire for revenge by introducing her to Scott Andrews. If he could manage that it would be well worth spending some time with him, even if he did give her the creeps. She wanted to know what sort of man Scott Andrews was. Going by Jolie's description he was a cross between Robert Redford and Superman. Leonie never took what Jolie said seriously, and always with a mammoth pinch of salt. She wondered if he had attended the funeral — not that she would have remembered. She hadn't known half of those paying their respects, she had been in too much of a daze.

She changed out of her tailored working suit, and chose to wear a pale cream slimline dress of soft angora wool. It was simple but tasteful, and hinted at more than it revealed. This she teamed with tan high heeled shoes and added a silk scarf which Jolie had bought her for her twenty-first birthday for further adornment. Not for the first time she thanked her lucky stars for having such a marvellous source of fashionable clothes to chose from, even if they weren't brand new.

She made a mental note to pay another visit to her friendly boutique. She could do with a new spring suit for when she had clients to visit, and she really must get another blouse, the one she had been wearing that day was becoming shabby and needed replacing. She felt first impressions mattered and always liked to retain a smart appearance, since one never knew when one would meet an important client — or Mr Right. The latter wasn't a high priority, but was always something to bear in mind.

Not bad she thought, twirling in front of the wardrobe mirror. She hoped Simon wouldn't think it was for his benefit that was all. She certainly didn't want to egg him on, this was a one off occasion because he had been so insistent. She supposed she owed him that much because of his kindness to her when Jolie died. He at least had been around and supportive in her hour of need when few others had.

He rang the doorbell a few minutes before the appointed hour. Leonie picked up her bag and went down to meet him, conscious that she was looking her best. Even her hair which she'd managed to pin up rather fetchingly was behaving for the time being.

His eyes lit up with admiration. "My, I hardly recognised you. You look quite ravishing! A proper little Cinderella."

Leonie's lips twitched — she was as tall as him, if not taller. No-one could call her little by any stretch of the imagination. "I wasn't sure where you had in mind."

"Can I tempt you to a meal? I haven't eaten yet. I know a great little restaurant. Chinese — you'll like it. We can make a night of it."

She was prepared for such a suggestion and had no intention of extending the outing. "Sorry, but I must get back by nine as I'm expecting a phone call.

Business must come first, I'm afraid."

His face fell. "Let's make best use of the next hour or so then. Perhaps another time," he joked reminding her of her usual excuse. After assisting her into the passenger seat of his ostentatious saloon he drove off, smoothly heading out of town. The car was the last word in luxury and refinement, which was probably what had attracted Jolie to him in the first place Leonie thought with a sigh. Jolie had loved the bright lights, the clubs, the discos and most of all men who would spend money on her.

"I thought we might pay the Flamingo Club a visit."

"That sounds fine," she said. "I don't believe I've ever been there." She had been with Jolie to quite a few night clubs just to please her friend and make up foursomes, but didn't get the same kick out of it as Jolie.

"It's where most of the local business community congregate. It hasn't been open long, but already it has quite a reputation as the in place to be."

Leonie knew that already and felt pleased that he'd suggested it. It wasn't the sort of establishment she felt she could go without an escort, and she had no boy friend at the moment. Jolie always badgered her to go out more — to socialise, but Leonie found her work occupied a great deal of her time. Not that she minded, she wasn't a gregarious sort of person and was quite satisfied with her own company. She knew that she ought to mix more as a means of securing new clients, but without her friend's coaxing and bullying she found it difficult. She contented herself with a quiet life. She missed Jolie dreadfully. The flat seemed so quiet these days — so tidy too!

The Flamingo Club was fairly busy but Simon found them seats and ordered her a martini and a lager for himself. To hear him ask for a non-alcoholic version intrigued her. She hadn't expected him to worry about the legality of drinking and driving.

"How's business?" he asked once their drinks arrived.

"Quite fair. Thanks mainly to you of course."

He looked gratified by her response.

"How about you?" she asked. "I don't even know what you do. I don't believe Jolie ever mentioned."

"Oh, a bit of this and a bit of that. I have financial interests in several local businesses, but mainly I specialise in the property market. If you're ever looking to buy a house or new offices let me know. I keep my ear to the ground and for you I'll make an extra special deal. After all, you might out grow your present premises before long if business keeps advancing."

"I'm not thinking of going anywhere for a while," she said with a slow smile. "One hears so many stories about the recession being over, but I'm still cautious. Thanks all the same. I'll keep you in mind for when, or if I ever do wish to expand. Do you know many of the people here?" There seemed to be lots of faces she recognised but couldn't put names to. Some were probably old friends of Jolie. Simon greeted many with a nod or a few words in passing.

"Sure. I know most of them. Quite a few are from Trenton not Chellow. I do a lot of business there these days. Trenton's growing fast with its new industrial estate. Their Council is more modern thinking and enterprising than Chellow's. They see and plan for the future and don't keep looking back at the past like the fuddy-duddys in Chellow Town Hall."

"Someone mentioned a Trenton firm to me only today. Now what was it." She pretended to rack her brains. "Ah yes, Andrews Electronics, that was it. Scott Andrews is the Managing Director. Is he here do you know?"

Simon looked around and shook his head. "Don't see him, but he often does drop in. Watch yourself if you tangle with him, he's pretty sharp. I tried to do a deal with him not so long ago but he turned me down flat. A most disagreeable fellow I found. His firm supplies electronic equipment all over the world. It's a thriving sector at the moment despite the recession, and one that I wouldn't mind investing in. His partner died recently and I thought I might jump in quick and buy his shares, but unfortunately Andrews was pretty astute and decided marriage to the beneficiary was the best option."

"That doesn't sound a very nice thing to do," Leonie said grimacing with distaste.

"Wheels of commerce, my dear Leonie, wheels of commerce. Not everyone marries for love in this day and age."

"Are you married?" Leonie asked deftly.

"Me! Good heavens, no. That's not my scene. Foot loose and fancy free that's me, and how I wish to remain. I don't want any woman tying me down, cramping my style."

Leonie wondered idly who would want to — certainly not herself. Soon a couple of local business men joined them and Simon made great play of introducing Leonie, making out that she was his current girl friend. She felt extremely annoyed and managed to extricate herself as best she could and went to the powder room at the first opportunity.

She took her time about renewing her make-up, spinning it out as long as possible. Eventually she wandered back into the lounge wondering whether she should call a taxi to take her home instead of waiting for Simon. She had done her duty and felt it was time to be making tracks because she didn't want him getting any crazy ideas about a repeat performance.

She was still considering the possibility of her means of escape as she negotiated her way through the maze of tables, when she stumbled and found herself face to face with a tall, well-dressed, Herculean individual. She quickly tried to side step him, annoyed by her carelessness, it wasn't like her to be so clumsy. Unfortunately, as quite often happens on these occasions they both stepped the same way. As their chests brushed Leonie felt a surge of electricity pass through her and she jumped back in shock. It quite took her breath away. She found herself frowning with annoyance.

The man gave her a lazy, coveted inspection then broke into a beaming, expressive smile. With a courteous mock bow he stood aside. "I'll gladly stand still if you would care to pass, or would you care to tango?" He held out his arms. "I'm sure you'd make an ideal dancing partner. Just the right height for me. It is a little crowded in here, though come to think of it that might make it all the more interesting."

"That's mighty kind of you," she replied with nod of approval as he eventually waved her through. She quickly slipped past and rejoined Simon who was still deep in conversation, but could feel 'Hercules' watching her and it brought the colour to her cheeks. His response to her clumsiness was most endearing and for a moment she wished he had taken hold of her as he'd suggested. The thought of dancing in his embrace made her head spin. She would like to have asked Simon who he was but couldn't find an opportunity to butt in.

"I'll have to go," she told Simon when she could get a word in edgewise. "I must be back in time for the phone call I told you about. I'll get a taxi, there's no need to interrupt your discussion."

"Wouldn't dream of it, my dear," he replied, gallantly getting to his feet. "No lady friend of mine goes home alone. I always see them back to their door. One never knows what wolves there are at large."

With lots of knowing smiles the meeting broke up. As Simon escorted her across the room his hand cupping her elbow, Leonie knew that 'Hercules' was still watching, even though she didn't see him. She could sense his eyes boring into her, and would love to have the nerve to turn and stare defiantly back, but she couldn't brazen it out. Her cheeks felt on fire, so she wouldn't give him the satisfaction of knowing that she found him attractive. His ego was already more than amply endowed without her adding to it. He had the air of confidence about him, as if he knew he stood out in any crowd. Vainglorious and egotistical she said to herself, definitely no shrinking violet.

2

BACK in Chellow Leonie hoped that she wasn't going to have trouble despatching Simon. By now he would be feeling hungry and she had no inclination to provide him with a snack even though she was peckish herself. She hinted that she had work to do and left it at that. She had arranged for Tina to ring at half past nine and make out she was an important client just in case, but as it turned out Simon accepted her story and dropped her off at the door with good grace. He seemed in good humour and didn't even try to make a pass at her for which she was extremely thankful. She thought there was nothing worse than fending off unwelcome approaches.

"It has been most enjoyable, Leonie. You made many conquests tonight which can't be bad. I'll call you again soon, OK? We must do this more often. I envisage already 'Girl Friday' becoming so successful and prosperous that you'll soon be moving into the Chellow Bank suite." He nominated the most prestigious office accommodation address in Chellow.

Leonie murmured dutifully. "Thank you for taking me. It made a nice change." Funnily enough she had enjoyed it she realised as she unlocked the front door and climbed the stairs to her flat. But also she felt decidedly uneasy — a premonition, although she wasn't sure why. Her female intuition was working overtime again probably.

She flopped down on the settee, kicked off her shoes and yawned hugely. It had been a long day but a reasonably rewarding one. Simon Dean was instantly forgotten having been completely overshadowed by the man she'd nicknamed Hercules. She just knew that their paths would cross again sometime. She could feel it in her bones, and the thought wasn't exactly unwelcome.

He'd been so impressive. Tall, broad shouldered and looked like a rugby player, with jet black, curly hair cut fashionably short. Thick, expressive eyebrows framed the most mesmerising blue eyes she had ever seen, and then the sensuously, kissable mouth. If she'd been an artist she could have drawn his face even though she had only seen it for a few moments.

He had made such an instant impression on her but she knew that he was quite out of her league. She thought what a strange mixture he'd evoked, of sterling strength yet compassion, determination but sensitivity and understanding, but overall an almost indescribable feeling of sensual masculinity. A marauding lion maybe? No — a panther she thought, a big black panther. That brought a smile to her lips as the phone rang and she stretched out lazily to answer it, automatically assuming it would be Tina.

"You left your scarf behind, Cinderella."

"I'm sorry. Who is this?" The voice was provocatively teasing and she could hear the deep masculine chuckle as she realised who she was speaking to. It had been the mention of Cinderella that had thrown her to start with — the second time that day. "How did you get my number?" she gasped. It felt almost as if she had spirited him into her living room merely by thinking about him. She immediately sat up and straightened her clothing.

"I rather thought you'd remember me — your dancing partner. Someone as eye-catching as you isn't hard to trace," he went on. "You livened up an otherwise dull evening. Shame you had to leave so soon."

"If you wouldn't mind popping the scarf in the post, I would be most grateful," Leonie stuttered, conscious of her heart thumping uncontrollably.

"I wouldn't want to lose it. It was a present."

Fancy him going to the trouble to learn who she was and where she lived she thought, pushing her hair out of the way so that she could hear better. He was obviously ringing from the club because she detected in the background the lively chit-chat and subdued music.

"I was thinking of delivering it personally. I wouldn't want it to get lost in the post. Is Dean still with you?"

"No, he most certainly isn't," she snapped.

"I'll be about twenty minutes."

The line went dead and Leonie stared at it for several minutes in total disbelief. When it rang again she almost jumped out of her skin.

"You all right, boss?" Tina asked. "You sound funny."

"Yes, yes," Leonie mumbled. "Sorry, I've got something on my mind. Thanks for ringing but it wasn't necessary thank goodness."

"No problem with our gallant friend then I gather? I'm sorry I was a bit late with the call but your line was engaged when I tried the first time." She paused for a moment. "See you in the morning then." Tina rang off leaving Leonie with the distinct feeling that she was miffed because she hadn't enlightened her about who she'd been talking to.

Leonie quickly tidied herself and plumped up the cushions for want of something to do. Her nerves were on edge. She walked backwards and forwards about the lounge like a schoolgirl waiting for her first date. "Pull yourself together," she berated herself. "He's only returning your scarf. You don't know anything about him. He's probably married anyway. Most likely passes through Chellow on his way back to wife and family. There's no need to invite him in. Just play it cool."

But she knew that she would ask him in if the occasion presented itself. She felt as if a spark of something exciting had been lit within her, something she'd never experienced before. She knew that the man was dangerous, he was far too confident and self assured for his own good, but that only made him more appealing in a way. Charisma Jolie would have called it. Some indescribable attraction which had Leonie all of a dither at the mere thought of having caught and held his attention. In the past many men had been attracted by the colour of her hair when they had gone out together, but it had been Jolie they had dated. Leonie hadn't been able to hold their attention next to her friend's lively personality. Now she was on her own. This time it would be different.

She heard the car pull up and couldn't resist peeping out of the window. She could tell as soon as she saw it that it was his. It suited his dynamic identity — a superb, racy sports model — speedy, expensive and eye-catching. It was a two seater which made her revise her earlier conjecture. Maybe he wasn't married after all. Maybe he was still fancy free and available, in which case —

He extricated himself from the car and glanced up with a thoughtful expression on his face, the scarf fluttering in the playful breeze. Leonie backed away hurriedly feeling embarrassed in case he saw her peeking. She didn't want him to get the impression that she was eagerly looking forward to meeting him again. When he rang the doorbell she leisurely counted to five before going to answer it.

"Thank you for your trouble," she said as soon as she opened the door. "I would hate to lose it. It's one of my favourites." She held out her hand for the scarf but he seemed loath to part with it.

"No trouble." He looked even more devastating standing on her doorstep, his gaze raking over her quite brazenly. It was an appreciative scrutiny though, not at all like Simon's. His eyes twinkled mischievously as if he knew the effect he had on her. "I wanted to meet you again anyway. This was a golden excuse."

"You did?" she frowned and cocked her head to one side.

"I've been hearing about the services you provide. I would like to hear more."

For some reason the way he said it — the tone of voice — a certain look — something made her angry. He made it sound somehow suggestive and immoral.

"I don't know what you've heard but I run a respectable secretarial agency." She pulled herself up to her full height, her eyes glinting stormily and tugged the scarf out of his hand. Being tall she looked him square in the face from her position one step higher than him.

"Hold on there." Holding up his hands in mock horror he backed away with an amused laugh. "I was referring to 'Girl Friday'. Maybe I could do with your assistance occasionally. Good secretaries are hard to find. When I asked around, some club members said you come highly recommended. Glowingly recommended I might add."

"Sorry," she said quietly, nibbling her lip. "I rather got the impression . . . "

"That's OK. A word of advice though. Simon Dean isn't the most sensible choice of escort about town. His reputation leaves a lot to be desired."

He didn't seem to be in a hurry to leave and it felt inappropriate to discuss business on the doorstep so Leonie opened the door wider.

"Would you care to come up?" automatically thinking that she should make the most of every opportunity to push her business venture. He looked the sort of man to have considerable influence in his field whatever it was, and she was always open to fresh offers. "I'm sorry but I don't even know your name."

She wasn't sure how she managed to walk back upstairs. When he mentioned who he was her legs began to quake uncontrollably. The coincidence was too much. It was like a bolt from the blue. She ought to have had some warning. Why hadn't Simon told her he had arrived at the club? Scott Andrews of Andrews Electronics — the very man she had wanted to meet. She led him into the lounge feeling as if a bombshell had exploded.

"Charming place you have. Convenient yet cosy." He strolled over to the window and peered down at his car. "Nice view too."

"I like it," Leonie replied, wondering if she'd taken leave of her senses. When he'd said who he was she should have shown him the door. She should never have invited him in like that. He'd toyed with Jolie's affections, and because of him Jolie was dead. If only Jolie hadn't missed the train . . .

She would like to ask how come he was still alive? How had he survived the crash and not his passenger? Since he was still alive, why hadn't he at least been at Jolie's funeral? Now that she had met him she knew he hadn't attended. There was no way she could have overlooked his presence. There had been no wreath or condolence note either. It was possible he had been in hospital she thought, but that wouldn't excuse everything.

Leonie could well understand how her friend could have fallen for him — but he wasn't going to do the same with her — not now that she knew who he was. At least she was fore-warned. He looked as if he was used to getting his own way, and she smiled inwardly wondering if he had any idea of her connection with Jolie, and how she had pledged to avenge her friend's death.

"Please, take a seat," she said in a calm, strained voice.

He waited until she sat down before taking over the only armchair she owned. He looked composed and comfortable as if he felt at home in the tiny apartment, while Leonie nervously pulled her skirt over her knees wondering what she was going to talk to him about. The room had become decidedly smaller and claustrophobic since his arrival, and she wished she'd taken him into the office so she could have the desk between them. She couldn't think why she hadn't done so. She never entertained clients in her private rooms.

"Have you been here long? Although we do have clients here I don't know Chellow all that well — not the town centre anyway. I'm from Trenton by the way. Andrews Electronics is on the new industrial estate. We recently moved from our original premises due to an increased work load."

Leonie smiled grimly. She knew that already. It had been that very morning that she'd gleaned that titbit of information. Wasn't it strange how coincidences occurred? All this time she had thought he was dead, and then within the space of twelve hours she had not only learned of his existence but met him too. She had been hoping that Simon would point him out to her so that she could observe him first, before being introduced to her adversary, and here he was introducing himself and clearly interested in her. This time there was no Jolie to distract him. She didn't think it was purely a business relationship he was seeking either from his tone. She tried to recall what Simon had said about him. Something about marrying his partner's sister. He sounded an absolute rake!

"I started 'Girl Friday' nearly three years ago," she told him, eager to converse on a safe subject, "but in those days I worked from a small bedsit here in Chellow. Then, two years ago I took out a lease on this property when business picked up. It was a gamble I suppose, but it paid off thank goodness."

"You seem to be doing very well in a short space of time. I congratulate you. It was an astute move I should think, your shop's in a prime position here in the town centre."

"A client told me about it initially and smoothed the way for me, otherwise I don't suppose I would have taken the chance. It's only small but adequate for the moment. It's been jolly hard work, and I still work long hours, but I think it's all been worthwhile. I quite like being my own boss."

"Despite the ups and downs?" He quirked one expressive eyebrow as if he understood. "I was curious about your association with Simon Dean. You two don't look as if you belong together, if you don't mind my saying so. You look far too sophisticated to be seen wining and dining with the likes of him."

She blushed. Not many men had spoken to her like that before. "Simon puts work my way," she admitted. "He's often asked me out for a drink or a meal, and on this occasion I found it difficult to refuse. He's a client that's all, he's not my boy friend."

"Hmm." He nodded. "You live alone I take it?"

"Yes. I do now."

"I'd best be going then." He got to his feet, winked audaciously. "I wouldn't want to ruin your reputation, or mine for that matter. I believe the Chellow residents are a self-righteous bunch on the whole. I have your number, so if I ever have need of secretarial services I'll know where to come in future. I take it that you have no objection to work from outside the Chellow area?"

"None whatsoever. In fact one or two of the girls I use live not so far from Tranton." Leonie hardly slept that night. Scott Andrews disturbed her dreams as well as her thoughts. She had wanted to meet him, and was determined to have her revenge, but he would prove to be an awesome opponent. She wasn't at all sure how she was going to get the better of him, but somehow she had to achieve it for Jolie's sake. Poor, poor Jolie.

Why did he have to be so devastatingly good looking? Now she knew why Jolie had said that he would appeal to

Leonie. At the time she had wondered if Jolie was matchmaking, since she had talked at length about this fantastic male she had met. Even as Leonie had berated her friend for thumbing a lift — something she had stressed on her never to do, Jolie had been irritatingly complacent. She had said quite confidently that she knew she was safe with him, and that Leonie would approve of her choicc when they met.

Safe? He would be a staunch defender of anyone he cared for she felt sure, and yes, she believed Jolie would have been safe with him. That made her wonder if he had already been engaged when he'd met Jolie.

* * *

For several days afterwards Leonie felt nervous every time the telephone rang expecting it would be him. She knew she was being totally irrational, but she knew it wouldn't be long before he found an excuse to employ her. Even

Tina noticed how jumpy she was and suggested that she needed a holiday, but a holiday was the last thing on Leonie's mind.

When Simon rang to ask her out she refused, pleading a heavy work load even though she had it under control. She didn't want to be seen out with him after what Scott had said, although she was curious about his reputation. Scott had intimated that he was perhaps slightly shady in his business dealings, which wouldn't altogether surprise her. Her first impressions were usually fairly accurate, but in Scott's case she felt biased by what she'd been told subsequently.

Scott, she murmured repeatedly. She knew she should be thinking of him as Mr Andrews, but she couldn't. Scott sounded so much nicer and more friendly. But I don't want to get friendly with him she told herself angrily. He's the enemy. He caused the death of Jolie, but she had a hard task reconciling the fact. She could still conjure up his face, and picture those kissable lips, and wish — wish that they were kissing her own. He was the first man to affect her in such a fashion, and she was annoyed to say the least that it should be him of all people.

* * *

It was ten days later that he finally got in touch. Leonie was about to go out to do some necessary shopping one Friday, when Tina buzzed on the intercom to say that a new client was on the phone and wished to speak to her personally. She knew before she asked who it would be. Sixth sense alerted her. A cold chill ran down her spine — a chill of suppressed excitement.

"Mr Andrews," she said brightly. "It's nice to hear from you. How may we help you?"

"For a start you can call me Scott, and I believe you told me your name was Leonie, right? Some day you'll have to tell me how you came to be christened with such an intriguing name. I haven't seen you at the club recently. I've missed you."

"I don't make a habit frequenting such places," she replied tartly, though satisfyingly pleased by his tantalising admission.

"Hmm, perhaps we could remedy that before long. But to business. I have a speech which I would like typed. It's confidential, and I gather from your card that is your watchword."

"That's correct, er . . . Scott. We at 'Girl Friday' pride ourselves on a highly efficient and trustworthy service. You can count on us."

"Good. I thought I'd try you out and see how you compare with your competitor in Trenton. I'll drop the tape off first thing tomorrow on my way to work. I need it for Monday evening. Is that too short notice?"

"No problem," she assured him blithely. Even if she had to stay up half the night she would have accepted the assignment. Leonie was in a quandary. She knew that having accepted the task she couldn't fail to live up to the high standard she expected from the rest of her employees, but on the other hand it was an ideal occasion to wreak her revenge. She mulled it over as she went for her weekly groceries, wondering how she could get retribution without it damaging the business. Revenge was one thing but she still had to survive. It would be stupid to throw away all that she'd built up, because nothing would bring Jolie back. She was so wrapped up in her thoughts that she returned to the flat with only half of what she had set out to purchase.

Suddenly, as she was putting away her shopping it came to her, and even though it may mean losing the odd client from Trenton she felt it would well be worth it. Mr Scott Andrews was going to have a difficult time on Monday evening if she had her way. 'Girl Friday' would live up to its reputation — that would be indisputable, but she realised that Scott Andrews wouldn't take kindly to the inconvenience, and would not be a regular customer in the future, more's the pity.

She found the tape in the letter box the next morning. Tina usually had Saturdays off unless there was a panic on, so this morning Leonie was looking after the shop herself. It wasn't a particularly busy morning, so she took time off to listen to the tape through once and assess how much time it would take her to transcribe it. It was a long speech, but he had a pleasing voice and the contents were witty and entertaining as well as informative. She felt sure it would go down well *if he ever gave it*!

Leonie worked all the next day on it even though it was Sunday. He said he didn't need it until Monday evening, but she wanted to make certain that she was prepared well in advance. She didn't want any slip ups — not this time. As usual, pride was at stake to provide the best possible service, and especially so on this occasion, so she double checked it through even after using the spell-checker.

On Monday morning as she entered the shop having made her delivery the phone was ringing. It was Tina to say that she felt unwell and wouldn't be in which meant Leonie would have to man the shop. It was as well she'd completed her assignment early she reflected, since Monday was often quite busy. In a way it suited her having the place to herself, since it gave her little time to think about what she had done.

In one way she felt elated that she had managed to score off Scott Andrews so quickly, but against that she knew that she could anticipate the full fury of his wrath. Whenever she thought about that she could feel her legs begin to buckle with trepidation. She had to keep reminding herself that if it hadn't been for Jolie she probably wouldn't have opened 'Girl Friday' in the first place. She had Jolie to thank for so many things.

By closing time Leonie was ready to put her feet up having had little time to relax all day. She also had a raging headache. Her head pounded as if taken over by a thousand drummers all trying to outdo the other. She knew it was caused by nerves and it wouldn't improve until late that evening, so there was little she could do but suffer in silence. She would like to have had a bath and a peaceful evening listening to music, but she knew that wasn't on the cards. At least not until much, much later. Maybe after Scott had been and she had told him exactly what she thought of him, then she could relax, until then there was nothing she could do but wait.

The phone rang as she was on her way upstairs. She hurried to the office to answer it, anticipating it would be Scott. She guessed he'd be worried about his speech which was quite understandable.

"It's about ready," she told him, fingers crossed. "As a new customer I want to make absolutely certain that you have no complaints so I'm having a final run through. I'll drop it off at the conference centre, so there's no need for you to make a detour. I have to go out anyway so it's no problem."

"That would be great," he replied. "It starts at eight, but I expect to be there by about seven-thirty which will give me time to familiarise myself with the text again. Maybe I'll see you there. Would you care to sit in? I could arrange it, and maybe we could have a drink afterwards?"

"No . . . no thank you," she stammered. "I have another appointment. I'm sorry."

"Pity," she heard him say before replacing the receiver using both hands as they shook so much.

Leonie hummed quietly to reassure herself, as she made some tea and settled to watch television in order to take her mind of what she had done.

She felt pleased but apprehensive too, wondering what Scott's reaction would be. She would love to be a fly on the wall at the meeting she thought, but then on second thoughts maybe not!

The telephone rang almost continuously from half past seven onwards, but she didn't answer it. At a quarter to eight she heard a car draw up outside and someone rang the doorbell rather insistently, but she studiously avoided seeing who it was. Eight o'clock came and then there was silence for a while, but it wasn't an easy silence.

She felt she couldn't go out, she had to wait in for the inevitable visitor. All she could do was pace the floor nurturing her grievance. For three hours she kept reminding herself of why she had done it. It was all for Jolie. Jolie would have been highly amused to know that serious, staid Leonie had put her business in jeopardy because of her. Leonie couldn't credit herself what she had done. It was most unlike her to be so irresponsible. If she could turn the clock back she knew she wouldn't have done anything so stupid, but the die was cast and she would have to live with the consequences.

As the evening wore on her nerves were stretched to the limit until it was almost unbearable. Her headache raged, and she felt almost sick with anxiety. It was nearly eleven o'clock when she heard the car screech to a halt outside. A car door slammed violently, then heavy footsteps pounded the pavement before someone stuck their finger on the bell push and kept it there. Slowly she went down to face him, knowing that it was going to be an extremely difficult confrontation.

"Hello. How did your speech go?" she asked innocently, summoning up a wan smile.

Instead of replying he simply barged open the door and hustled her up the stairs before exploding. Yanking her by the arm he sat her down on the settee and stood guard over her. He was absolutely livid with rage.

"Explain yourself," he snapped. His eyes glaring into hers only inches away were the colour of blue ice and unequivocally menacing.

"Didn't you get your speech?" she asked smugly, determined not to give way to his intimidatory tactics, despite her heart thumping like a jack hammer.

He looked startled by her apparent calmness, and in a pique of anger strode over to the window, rubbing the back of his neck. He shook his head as if mystified by her behaviour.

"Maybe if I told you that I am Jolie's sister you will understand," Leonie said softly, massaging her arm which he'd held in such a vice-like grip. She would have a bruise there tomorrow.

He looked even more bewildered. "I don't know anyone of that name," he snapped.

Leonie blinked and sucked in a deep breath. "Jolene Jones. JJ she often called herself. Surely you must remember her! It's not *that* long ago. Once seen never forgotten. She told me all about you.

How wonderful you were. How kind you had been to give her a lift, and how it had been love at first sight for both of you. I know Jolie was excitable, but this time — this time — It was such a whirlwind affair that she was even talking about getting married . . . next month . . . "

"I've had enough of your petty games," he growled storming over towards her again, and suddenly she felt seriously vulnerable. She was alone in the flat with an incensed angry tiger who looked as if he was intent on shaking the life out of her. She knew there was no-one in hearing distance if she screamed, since nobody lived in the properties round about, they were all purely commercial businesses. She realised that she shouldn't have let him in, but it was too late now for such considerations.

She stood up, nervously biting her bottom lip, extremely scared, but reluctant to let him see her dilemma. She had gone this far so she had to see it through. Turning abruptly she took a photo-frame off the sideboard and handed it to him. There were tears in her eyes as she thrust it under his nose.

"That was Jolie, in case you have so many lady friends that you need to refresh your memory. She died in the road accident three months ago. Now do you recognise her?"

He glanced at it casually. "I've never set eyes on her before I tell you."

Leonie's hand shook as she replaced the photograph. His sharp retort caused her a moment of panic. "I suppose I expected you to say that," she said, tilting her head up to stare angrily at him. "Did she mean so little that you couldn't even send a few flowers as a farewell gesture? You see she 'phoned me the night before she died, and told me all about you. She thought you were the next best thing to sliced bread, and yet all the time you had a girl friend back in Trenton. I tried to warn her, but . . . You let her believe . . . "

"Where was I supposed to have met this infant?" he interrupted.

"Jolie would have been nineteen next month. That's an old photograph. Shall I refresh your memory still further?" Leonie's lips curled in disgust. "Remember your last skiing trip?"

"Skiing trip? Three months ago?" Scott's forehead furrowed deeply, clearly mystified.

"Early in January. Jolie was to have met up with a group of friends, but instead she was with you. She told me it had been great — the best holiday she ever had because she had finally fallen in love. She rang me on the last night of her holiday to tell me that she was coming back by car — with you. Naturally I assumed you'd both been killed, until I saw an article in the paper about you generously donating a computer to the local hospice. What happened? Did you forget to tell Jolie that you were already spoken for?"

"And where precisely was I supposed to have been skiing?" he demanded growing angrier by the minute.

"Scotland of course, where else?"

"Miss Davis, it may interest you to know that I have not been to Scotland for years, I have never met your sister, and for your information whenever I go skiing I prefer to go to Austria not Scotland."

Leonie stared at him. He seemed so emphatic that she found herself automatically believing him. He wasn't just saying it to absolve himself of Jolie's death, he meant every word. "I don't understand . . . " She slumped down. Her legs seemed to have turned to jelly, and she felt the colour draining from her face at the enormity of what she had done. If he was innocent — it was too appalling to contemplate.

"Neither do I, but that is beside the point," he growled. "I want to know where my speech is? So much for your efficient service, Miss Davis."

"It is where it is supposed to be," she said slowly, her mind on other things. If he wasn't who she thought he was, then . . . "I delivered it personally first thing this morning. I never like to let my clients down, and in your case I made a special effort. I worked all yesterday on it."

"I don't believe you. I had everyone hunting high and low, but it was not to be found. I had to rely on my memory and a few scribbled notes. I could wring your pretty little neck."

"I'm sorry," she said. "I have a copy here which I'll show you . . . "

"That's a fat lot of good now. I'll make you pay for this, young woman. You'll not make a monkey out of me and get away with it."

"I don't understand . . . " Leonie kept repeating herself as if in a fog of confusion.

"I can see that," he snarled. "What pray are you going to do to rectify your mistake?"

"What do you suggest?" she whispered.

He glared first at the photograph and then at Leonie. "I'll be in touch." He looked as if he was having great difficulty in containing his anger. He crashed out of the flat slamming the outside door so forcefully that the whole building seemed to shake.

Leonie huddled on the settee clutching a cushion for comfort, listening to the roar of the exhaust as he drove away. What had she done! Whatever had she done? His anger was defensible if what he said was true, and she shuddered at what form his retribution would take.

What if he broadcast to everyone just how she'd let him down, she'd go out of business in no time, especially if Simon also took offence at her rebuff. She couldn't understand how she'd made such a horrendous mistake. Jolie had been so excited — babbling on about this wonderful man she'd met, and even though the line had been poor Leonie was positive that she'd got the name correct. 'Scottie' she'd affectionately called him. That had been clear enough.

3

FOR three whole days Leonie was a nervous wreck waiting for the axe to fall. She didn't think it would be long before Scott Andrews devised a plan to get even with her. He wasn't the sort of individual who would take kindly to a woman getting the better of him she felt sure, even if it had been a genuine mistake. Her apologies went unheeded.

It was still a complete mystery as to how she had been misled in the first place. She was always so careful and precise. The only thing she could think was that Jolie in her excitement hadn't enunciated clearly with so much background noise.

Scott telephoned her one evening, long after Tina had left for home. Leonie wished she'd had the fore thought to put the answerphone on, but she hadn't anticipated him calling out of office hours. It had never occurred to her, and when the phone rang she immediately thought it would be one of the women who worked for her; they often phoned in the evening to let her know they were available if she needed them.

As soon as she heard the crisp voice barking instructions down the line, she closed her eyes as if by not seeing him she could shut him out. It was no use, the tirade bombarded her ears, and she could visualise him quite clearly — his arctic eyes and menacing stance. At no time did he give her an opportunity to apologise again, which she was more than ready to do.

"Still prepared to make amends?"

"Yes," she replied as firmly as she could. "Yes of course. I promised . . . "

"You are to accompany me on a business trip then, Miss Davis. I'll pick you up at seven sharp on Monday morning. Be ready and have your passport available. I presume you do have a current one?"

"Yes," she said gulping nervously, completely mesmerised by his curt demands.

"What . . . where . . . what else do I . . . "

"We are flying to Austria, and we will be staying overnight."

Leonie was left hanging on to the phone long after he had replaced the receiver. She was stunned by his imperious ultimatum. He hadn't given her any opportunity to explain why she couldn't possibly go abroad with him at such short notice. It had been a directive to be ignored at her peril.

For the rest of the evening she mutinously declared that she couldn't possibly accede to his wishes, and he couldn't force her to go. Who did he think he was? The way he talked one would think they were back in the middle ages. Did he really believe he could browbeat her into submission like that? She had agreed to make amends — yes, but assumed it would be a local commitment, not one hundreds of miles away.

Several times she took up the phone to call him back, but she couldn't bring herself to dial the number, and eventually weakly accepted that she should accept the assignment as retribution and that would be the end of it. She assumed he needed someone to take dictation, and perhaps type up a report of some meeting or other which shouldn't prove too onerous surely, with a trip to Austria thrown in for good measure. If she went about it the right way maybe she could even enjoy the trip — she had never been to Austria before.

Once she had been asked to attend a seminar with a client, but that had been in Birmingham, and he had been an elderly gentleman who in truth wanted her as his chauffeur. A trip abroad in the course of business was unheard of, so she smiled at the prospect of visiting another country and being paid to do so. She paused for a moment wondering if she would get paid, but then realised that he would have to pay for the flight tickets and the hotel accommodation, so even if she wasn't paid anything for her time it would be worth it.

* * *

Monday morning arrived. "You travel light I see — remarkable for a woman. Get in. Give me your case and I'll put it in the boot."

"I was about to say that I can't possible accompany you. I have commitments . . . "

His eyebrows rose marginally as he opened the passenger door. "So have I. Get in, you're going with me if you value your livelihood. You had better start living up to your reputation."

Leonie climbed in. It had been a half hearted attempt at refusal. She hadn't expected him to back down, and she refused to reveal how scared she felt by his dictatorial tone. He looked even larger than life this morning. After stowing her case he took his seat behind the wheel glowering his displeasure. He wore the same dark pin-stripe suit he'd worn at the Flamingo Club, only this time his shirt was snowy white, accentuating his tanned skin. His tie was what Leonie would describe as jazzy, and she guessed it had been a gift from some doting member of his family or girl friend maybe. She caught a whiff of subtle aroma — not aftershave but a clean fresh-from-the-shower raw masculinity. One only had to look at him to know that he meant business.

"My usual clients have more . . . "

"I am not one of your usual clients though, am I? For the next two days you will do as I say if you want to wipe the slate clean — got it?"

Leonie sat biting her tongue and strained to keep as much distance between them as possible, which was exceedingly difficult in the close confines of the car's compact interior. Over the weekend she had dithered with excitement. If it was supposed to be retribution it was taking a strange form. He would probably be extremely critical of her shorthand and typing capabilities she knew, but she was confident about her expertise on that score for it not to worry her. Under pressure she could usually shut everything else out and concentrate on the work in hand, so this would be good practice. The time spent travelling may be a bit of a strain, but if she simply remained calm and kept her mouth shut he would no doubt soon get tired of his own voice.

She considered arranging for one of her employees to accompany him, but she knew that wouldn't have worked. He expected her. It was herself that he was seeking to punish, and she couldn't inflict him on anyone else. Inflict, she thought wryly, was a strange word for what could be a wonderful experience on the right occasion with the right man. When they first met she had thought he might just be Mr Right, but not any more — not after such a faux pas.

"Hope you've brought something eye-catching," he remarked, casually glancing at her smart, apple green suit and pale lemon blouse. She had deliberated for quite some time about what would be appropriate, considering the possibility of snow even in Austria. She gathered from his nod that her outfit met with his approval, but she didn't know whether to be pleased or repelled by his inspection. As usual she had dressed with care, and the suit, though simple obviously had an expensive price tag.

"I trust I have all that is required," she murmured staring blindly ahead.

He sniffed as if amused by her response. "You have all the requirements I assure you. I expect people are often taken in by your apparent innocence. Most men are gullible when it comes to a beautiful woman, so you can turn on your charm when we meet my client."

"That is not the sort of work I do, Mr Andrews," she said frostily. "You may as well know . . . "

He sighed. "Get this straight, Miss Davis, if you want to keep your business running then you'd best do as I say. Dean isn't the only one with contacts you know. A few well chosen words in the right ears . . . "

After that he drove speedily towards the airport and Leonie lapsed into mutinous silence again. It was going to be the longest two days of her life by the look of things. So much for enjoying the trip, but she knew she only had herself to blame.

At the airport he hustled her through the formalities and then spent the next couple of hours delving into his brief case and reading paperwork, completely ignoring her. Leonie knew that there was no way she could walk out, so she bought a magazine and sat turning the pages a little distance away. She would love to know exactly where they were going and who they were going to see, but she was determined not to ask. All would be revealed eventually so she may as well accept what fate had in store.

She made one call to the office to leave a message on the answering machine informing Tina which flight she was on. She felt someone ought to know of her whereabouts. The previous Friday Tina had tried to prise more information from her, but Leonie adamantly refused to give her any. There wasn't much more she could tell her anyway, and she felt embarrassed by the whole scenario.

Despite his apparent detachment Leonie sensed Scott watching her, as if coldly assessing her capabilities just like he had at the Flamingo Club, so whenever their eyes met she stared rebelliously back. She wished she could go back in time — she wished she had never jumped to such a stupid assumption. Why hadn't she checked more thoroughly? It had all happened so alarmingly quickly that she hadn't behaved rationally at all. If only . . .

* * *

The two hour flight was a golden opportunity for Leonie to close her eyes and pretend to sleep. She was tired, she would love to sleep but sleep evaded her. After having had several poor nights she felt decidedly lethargic, but *his* proximity caused her too much tension to relax sufficiently. Flying didn't bother her one iota but his closeness definitely did. She couldn't forget their first meeting no matter how hard she tried, and despite all that had happened since she still felt that fatal electrifying attraction. She hadn't yet worked out exactly what it was that held her with such fascination, all she knew was that he had brought discord to her otherwise peaceful existence. Life was never going to be the same again.

They landed at midday and then had a long drive to Innsbruck by hire car. Since it was the first time Leonie had visited the country she looked about eagerly, finding the landscape both impressive and scenic. She watched the changing countryside in silence, enjoying for the moment being away from Chellow and the strain of running her business. What problems that arose which Tina couldn't deal with would have to wait until she got back, so there was no point in worrying about them. She was making a supreme effort to remain calm.

Scott too seemed relaxed and content to drive leisurely to their destination. She did wonder momentarily if it was for her benefit so that she could admire the scenery, but then recognised how silly that concept was. They were there on business and she was along so that he could seek retribution not take her on a sight-seeing trip. Obviously there was no urgent appointment that day, although he hadn't told her yet when her services would be needed.

Mulling over her position, Leonie reflected on how comparatively safe she felt in Scott's presence, despite his obvious anger with her. If it had been anyone else she would probably have refused point blank to be intimidated into leaving the country — especially in the company of an almost complete stranger. Business or not she wasn't one to behave irresponsibly, at least not normally. She liked to have her plans well formulated and itemised. This trip was totally unreal, and yet she knew Jolie would have approved. Jolie had been right about that — she definitely felt safe with him. Then she remembered, it hadn't been Scott she was referring to.

They stopped for lunch in a small village, and while they waited for their meal Scott asked her about Jolie. At first Leonie was reluctant to say much — he wouldn't understand. How could he?

"I first met Jolene when I was sent to a children's home. Jolie and I shared a bedroom. I was nine and she was six — a very precocious and friendly six year old I remember. We became inseparable, and shared many hare-brained experiences during our time there — usually at Jolie's instigation of course."

"You have no family?"

"No," Leonie murmured, nibbling her bottom lip. "Neither of us had. Jolene's mother wasn't married and unfortunately she died in childbirth. Jolie lived all her life in the children's home, but she was remarkably resilient and coped with the life better than I did. She was always prepared to have a go at anything. She used to say that life was for living to the full since one never knew how long one had been allotted. I've since wondered if she was thinking about her mother, or if she foresaw her own short life-span."

"It must have been tough for you — both of you, I can see that. I'd like to have met Jolene. She sounds to have been a lively companion."

The meal arrived and they ate in silence, Leonie conscious of her incoherent thoughts. She was attracted to him and yet everything she heard suggested that she should be repelled by him. She kept thinking back to their first meeting — before she even knew his name. He had instinctively appealed to her, and at the time she surmised that he felt the same about her. Could her first impression be so wrong? But there was still the question of his fiancée.

* * *

Scott eventually drew up outside a modest looking hotel on the outskirts of Innsbruck. It appeared to be busy with many people coming and going, and Leonie heard snatches of conversation in assorted languages. She was fascinated with the whole atmosphere and felt herself relaxing, it was such a typical holiday scene. Snow graced the mountain tops, but down in the town it was pleasantly warm and sunny.

Scott motioned her to lead the way and they entered the hotel foyer. Leonie, head held high walked towards the reception desk.

"Good evening, Mr and Mrs Andrews. Your room is on the second floor." The manager smiled obsequiously and handed Scott the key. "I hope you enjoy your stay."

Leonie stared in horror. Now she realised why Scott wished her to accompany him. Her feet simply refused to move, they seemed to be glued to the spot. For a moment she couldn't even find her voice. A red mist swam before her eyes. There was no way she would agree to such a proposition.

"I can't . . . "

"We'll use the lift. This way."

With his holdall and her case in one hand he hauled her away before she had time to remonstrate too loudly. Leonie was fuming, but couldn't bring herself to cause a scene in the entrance with all the other guests milling around, but as soon as they entered the lift which was fortunately empty, she turned on him.

"I won't share a room with you. That isn't . . . "

He merely pushed the relevant button which sent the lift speeding on its way, and placidly leaned back against the panelling. He appeared totally unconcerned by her outburst. "You will," he remarked evenly "because there aren't any other rooms available. There's a music festival on and everywhere is fully booked."

The lift arrived at the second floor and the doors opened. Leonie mutely stumbled out as if in a dream — or a nightmare, Scott hustling her along the corridor like a recalcitrant child. He unlocked the door of their room and urged her inside.

"I'm surprised at you making such a fuss," he snapped.

"I don't believe this is happening," Leonie said, wearily slumping down on to one of the chairs. She was nearly in tears. Safe, she thought dismally, she'd been thinking she was safe with him. How wrong could she be? Caged up with a man-eating tiger in a foreign country; she simply didn't know how to handle it.

"Why?" she sobbed. "I did type your speech as requested, and delivered it on time. I kept my side of the bargain. You've no right to . . . "

"You forgot to mention that it was in a chocolate box and beribboned like a birthday present!"

"You didn't ask." She snuffled.

He threw the bags on to the bed with a growl. "Well, you had your little joke at my expense, so now I'll have mine. Unpack and I'll see you downstairs. I've got a busy day tomorrow. I'll be in the bar. Pull yourself together and maybe we'll be able to enjoy a civilised dinner together."

Immediately he left she rang down to reception to enquire if there was another room available. She would have taken any they had — anything at all to get out of the present predicament, but they apologised saying the hotel was indeed fully booked, as were most of the hotels in the area. They didn't know of a vacancy to be had anywhere. They were most apologetic and she had to pacify them most profusely, admitting that there was nothing wrong with the room.

It was too late now to leave Leonie realised. Even if she returned to the airport Scott had their tickets and she had doubts about getting another flight. Leonie set about unpacking her case and hung up the blouse and two dresses which she'd brought with her, wondering how she should best cope with the situation. She hadn't known what to pack since she didn't know what Scott's plans were. Now she did and she was far from happy.

She had a shower hoping that it would somehow make her feel better, but every time she looked at the double bed her heart almost stopped. Granted it had two single mattresses and separate duvets, but the bed was still all in one piece — totally inseparable. She couldn't possibly sleep there next to him. She wouldn't dare close her eyes. The only alternative was an old armchair, which had seen better days and didn't look too comfortable but might be the inevitable solution.

She dispiritedly changed into a peach and brown boldly patterned dress and piled her hair up as best she could, before venturing to unpack Scott's holdall as instructed. She wasn't sure why she was being so obliging in view of his autocratic attitude, but went ahead anyway. The clean shirt ought to be put on a hanger overnight to rid it of its creases. He travelled light so it didn't take long, but she went white with horror when she realised that there were no pyjamas — just a spare shirt and dressing gown, etc. She wondered what he intended wearing in bed — surely he didn't sleep in the nude! The nightmare was getting worse by the minute.

Eventually she felt that she had spent as much time as she dare and would have to go downstairs or else he would come looking for her — that was the last thing she wanted. The thought of being alone in the bedroom with him terrified her. She had the sneaking suspicion that if he turned on the charm like he had at the Club she wouldn't be able to resist his advances, and she felt far too unworldly to cope with that right now.

"There you are. I was beginning to wonder if you'd run out on me. What will it be, Martini?" He seemed to have recovered his temper, and even managed a wry smile of welcome.

"Thank you," she said coldly, glancing round at the rest of the residents in the room. She wondered what they thought. Did they see them as a married couple, or did they suspect the truth?

"You took your time, but it was worth it I see. You look simply marvellous. I don't know how you manage to buy such fabulous clothes. Business must be doing well."

"I manage," she said quietly. She

didn't see why she should explain or justify her position to him, so let him think what he liked.

"I can well imagine." He seemed to find great pleasure in teasing her with double meanings. "By the way I should tell you that in future I won't have you consorting with Simon Dean. He's history as far as you are concerned. Got it?"

"You can't dictate to me who I go out with," Leonie retorted with spirit. "I'm a free agent, so I do as I please. You don't own me, Mr Andrews. Simon has been very kind to me in the past and put a lot of business my way."

"I mean it, Leonie," he growled. "I detest the man."

Leonie remained tight lipped. She didn't like Simon any more than he did, but she wasn't going to have him telling her who she could go out with. It was none of his business.

"The feeling's mutual I gather. He said the same about you."

"Been discussing me behind my back have you?"

Leonie realised too late that she'd ɔken out of turn. "He just happened , mention you in passing, but I got .he impression that he didn't like you. How did you offend him?"

Scott nodded to the barman to order the drinks before replying. "Dean had the gall to approach me about buying into my company only a couple of weeks after my partner was killed. I hadn't come to terms with the new situation, it had been such a body blow, and in he waltzed suggesting he step in just like that. I was thunderstruck at his temerity, and felt like punching him to kingdom come for his lack of tact and decency. He's the most ill-mannered weasel I've every had the misfortune to come across. Anyway, for your information I am taking over where he left off. If you need more business put your way then I'll do it, if you play your cards right that is. You don't need the likes of him around."

"You are doing this for revenge aren't you?" she said quietly. "It isn't simply because of what I did. You are using me as an excuse to get back at him."

"Yes, in a way. Andy was a good friend as well as my partner. I won't have an upstart like Dean anywhere near our company. If I needed money he would be the last person I'd go to. The nerve of the man defies belief."

"What happened to your partner?"

Scott's face closed and he twirled the liquid idly round in his glass. When he spoke his voice was low and subdued. "He went to Glencoe to stay with friends for an extended holiday. He'd been working damned hard and deserved a break. He'd just landed us a big contract with an Australian company and I thought I was doing him a favour when I volunteered to visit the client instead of him. What a mistake that turned out to be!" He gave a long sigh and rubbed the back of his neck seemingly lost in thought.

"It's something I'll never forget to my dying day. I keep going over again and again, if only . . . " He paused again. "On the way south Andy was involved in an accident. His car collided head on with a coach which crashed through the central reservation on the motorway. The weather was simply appalling I gather, and he was killed outright. That was the one thing I was thankful for, he probably never knew what hit him.

"It was a horrendous mess by all accounts but it was so unfair. Andy was an exceptionally good driver and never one to take chances. He was a rally driver in his spare time for goodness sake. I'm clear in my own mind that it was in no way his fault. I suppose he just happened to be in the wrong place at the wrong time and for that he can blame me."

Leonie stared at him horror-struck. "When exactly did this happen?"

"The tenth of January to be precise." He looked at her quizzically. "Are you thinking what I'm thinking?"

She nodded, unable to speak.

He went on. "My partner's name was Andy. Andrew Scot. We got to know each other at University because of the similarity in our names. People kept muddling us up. It was Andy that Jolie met wasn't it? It's all beginning to make sense."

"Andrew Scot. Scottie," Leonie repeated slowly, and closed her eyes realising her own stupidity.

"Many people called him Scottie because of his accent. He was of Scottish descent while am as English as they come. In a way we were like chalk and cheese. I believe someone told me he'd picked up a hitch hiker now I come to think of it. I guess that was your — Jolie. Your mention of skiing threw me because that was one sport Andy and I didn't share. He tried it once but found he couldn't master the technique to be really proficient so that was that as far as he was concerned. If he couldn't become an expert in anything he preferred not do it at all. He was a bit of a show-off.

"He was a year younger than me but had a far more outgoing personality. He did most of the selling while I looked after the work in progress. Andy could have talked Eskimos into buying refrigerators, he was that sort of guy, but he was hopeless with paperwork. That was why we made a great team. It really shook me when I learned he was dead, he was such a live wire, full of daring exploits and fun. I still can't believe it. I didn't arrive back in the country in time to attend the funeral even — I couldn't get a flight."

Leonie didn't know what to say. "I am sorry," she said eventually. "I seem to have made a dreadful mess of things. It's not like me but . . . I suppose at the time I wasn't thinking too clearly. I must have mis-heard or something. It was all so appalling . . . but . . . well . . . I honestly thought it was you Jolie meant, and when I saw that you weren't dead after all — I was angry to say the least. She sounded so thrilled. She had really fallen in love this time, and when someone said you were engaged . . . I simply saw red and knew I had to hit back — for her sake." Blinking back tears Leonie took a sip of her drink, trying not to recall the horror of that dreadful time.

"I suppose in the circumstances I can understand," Scott murmured. "I felt like punching someone when I heard about the accident too. However, I didn't appreciate the manner in which you went about it, my girl. You made me look a complete fool, stumbling over my speech like that. That is something I won't tolerate. I do make mistakes — everybody does, but I prefer them to be of my own making and then I'll take full responsibility for them."

"Jolie was all I had. We were like sisters, but I don't suppose you would understand," Leonie said biting her lip to stop the tears forming.

He sighed and covered her hand with

his, giving it a commiserating squeeze. "I'm so sorry. It must have been an especially bitter blow for you. I can't imagine what it must be like to have no relatives — not that they are all a blessing I hasten to add. Anyway, who told you I was engaged? It wasn't in the papers."

"I don't remember. Why?"

"Oh, no reason."

"Have you any family," she asked trying her best not to get emotional, but the light contact made her heart leap. Every time he touched her she felt that spark. When he let go she felt a little bereft.

"I have a doting, grey haired mother and a dotty sister who is married to a vet."

"And a fiancée too," she reminded him primly.

"Yes, as you say, and a fiancée too, but that's another story." He grimaced, shrugged his shoulders and stood up. "Drink up and let us go into dinner. I think we should have an early night. I want you bright eyed and bushy tailed tomorrow."

The mention of an early night completely ruined Leonie's appetite. Her stomach muscles tensed at the thought of sharing that double bed with him. He was so incredibly attractive and if they had met under different circumstances she would have enjoyed his company very much. At the Flamingo Club she had felt an instant, strong attraction for him which still persisted, but now it was tempered with fear too. Fear at her erratic feelings towards him and fear of what he expected from her. The whole episode was becoming more unreal by the minute.

"Tell me what made you start up in business?" he asked while they waited for the soup course. "It was quite a gamble wasn't it at your age, with no family to support and encourage you?"

Leonie, recognising his attempt to calm things, accepted the olive branch.

She couldn't spend all evening in silence which was what she had intended doing. He had lost someone close too so she knew how he felt.

"When I left school I got a job in an office and decided to better myself by taking night classes on typing, shorthand, word processing and bookkeeping, but it all came to nought when I was made redundant." She grimaced. "I felt I had nothing to lose by having a go at becoming self-employed, starting in a small way. I had my qualifications, and to begin with a trusty old typewriter, later replaced by a computer.

"It surprised me how quickly things took off. I put an advert in the local paper and soon I found that I had more work than I could cope with. However, I hated the idea of turning anyone down in case they wouldn't come back again, but I didn't feel comfortable employing others on a formal basis. I was only nineteen and had heard such stories about over-extending — and growing too quickly. The work load fluctuated quite a lot. I thought it too much to risk employing anyone permanently, so I approached some of my former work mates. Mostly married women happy to earn some pocket money working freelance and hours aren't a problem."

"Sounds a promising situation. So why the connection with Dean then?"

"He was a friend of Jolie's. After the funeral he kept in touch — the only one of her friends to do so. He knows most of the local business men in Chellow, and as my business expanded he put my name forward, arranging for several of them to use my services from time to time. In such a small community it's who you know that counts in many cases."

"You expect me to believe that is all there is between you? Pigs might fly. Dean's a most undesirable character. I know his game. Everyone at the club knows too," Scott said in an exasperated tone.

"I don't particularly like him, but I can't afford to lose his custom." She glared back angrily, and then realised that people nearby were beginning to stare in their direction. Deliberately she changed the topic of conversation. "What do you do anyway? From what Simon said you deal world-wide in electronics, whatever that might mean."

"Correct. Tomorrow, we are meeting a client, Giorgio Sterne who I hope will order large quantities of our specialised chips."

"And you want me to take notes of the meeting?"

"Hmm. You might also use your feminine wiles to best advantage to oil the wheels. I believe Giorgio is still a happy bachelor."

She drew in deeply determined not to cause a scene. It took a great deal of self discipline not to get worked up and walk out, but somehow she coped. Jolie, she knew, would have thrown the soup over him and not cared a jot. Unfortunately she wasn't like Jolie, but how she wished she were right now.

"Tell me about your partner. What was he like?"

Once they got on to safe ground talking about Andy and Jolie the conversation wasn't quite so acrimonious and she managed to make the evening last longer than she dared hope. Soon after half past ten though he looked at his watch. "I'll give you ten minutes to get ready, OK?"

Leonie snatched up the key, scurried up to the bedroom and locked the door. She had made up her mind what she was going to do during dinner. What he would do when he found out she wasn't sure. He'd probably not want to make too much commotion and alert the whole hotel, on the other hand she didn't expect him to meekly accept the situation. Should she leave him one of the duvets outside the door so that he could sleep in the car? It would serve him right if he caught his death of cold!

Quickly she removed her make

up and got ready for bed feeling apprehensive but determined. She was sitting at the dressing table brushing her hair when suddenly she doubled up in pain. For a moment she could scarcely breath as her stomach churned and became almost rigid with sharp spasms of intolerable discomfort. She made it to the bathroom — just, and was being violently sick when she heard Scott arrive outside the door.

"Leonie," he called, rattling the door handle. "Leonie, let me in." He sounded at first merely irritated but then angry.

She couldn't move, she daren't move. She couldn't care less what he did, where he went, or if he broke the door down even. He could rouse the rest of the residents for all that she cared, she had problems of her own. Dimly she heard other voices outside and then shortly afterwards he burst into the bathroom.

"You all right?" He was quick to appraise the situation, she gave him credit for that. She felt the cool damp cloth on her forehead and his comforting arm around her shoulder, and accepted his ministrations with genuine gratitude. She wasn't conscious of her scanty attire, who he was or what was happening. She felt so dreadful that she just wanted to curl up and die.

He almost carried her to the bed, his manner solicitous and gentle. "You'll be all right with a good night's sleep. Can I get you anything?"

She stared up at him white faced and shivering, speechless with misery and shook her head.

"Come on, hop in." He helped to remove her dressing gown and threw it on to the nearest chair. "You sleep nearest the bathroom in case of need." He held up the duvet and she slithered under it thankfully. She hoped she wasn't going to be sick again, and if she kept perfectly still maybe the nausea would pass. She made a conscious effort to try to relax, but it wasn't easy with Scott around.

She heard him in the bathroom and he emerged wearing his dressing gown but she saw his bare legs as he walked past. Sanity was reasserting itself as she felt him get in at his side, but by then she was grateful for the comfort of the mattress and couldn't bring herself to swap it for the armchair. For the moment she felt reasonably safe.

"Goodnight, Leonie. I hope you'll feel better in the morning." He switched off the light and shuffled down with a deep sigh which to Leonie sounded like a groan.

The darkness was a blessed relief and she lay awake for a long time hardly daring to move in case she disturbed him. She was conscious of every slight movement he made. Nothing was going according to plan. Finally she managed to sleep, but it was a somewhat troubled sleep. She tossed and turned as demons pursued her. One of her old familiar nightmares returned to haunt her. It always seemed so real — so horrifyingly real. She watched in horror as the car disappeared over the cliff. She wanted to scream — she tried to scream but nothing came out, and then she was alone. All alone and extremely frightened.

* * *

"Are you feeling better this morning?"

Leonie woke to find Scott sitting up in bed watching her. She couldn't look into his eyes, she was feeling far too embarrassed, but stared at the mass of dark hair covering his expansive chest. She wondered what it must be like to bury her head against it, that matt of soft springy curls looked most inviting, and she shivered with anticipation.

"Yes, thank you," she gulped raking her hair back off her face. "Much better."

He folded his arms exposing well developed muscles all hard and sharply defined.

"Do you realise the sun shining through a crack in the blinds is lighting up your hair like a halo. You look like an angel, but I suspect you deliberately locked me out last night. Why?"

"Why do you think? I told you all along, I'm not . . . not one of those sort of women. I don't know what gave you the idea that I . . . "

"Are you trying to tell me that all the rumours about you are totally unfounded?" he asked clearly disbelieving her.

"What rumours? Who's been talking about me? I'll have you know that I have never been to bed with a man before in my life. So you can . . . can . . . " she finished with a sob. She hadn't meant to tell him how green she was, how totally inexperienced and shy she felt. At her age it was most unusual she knew, and she felt somewhat ashamed to have to admit it.

Scott continued to stare at her as if seeing her for the first time. He seemed genuinely fazed. Finally, shaking his head he began chuckling, then he threw back his head and laughed out loud. This startled Leonie, making her angry. She couldn't see what was so amusing. She sat up pulling the duvet round her and hugged her knees, waiting until his laughter died down.

"I'm glad you find the situation amusing, because I must say I don't."

"I was laughing at myself actually," he said. "I'm sorry, truly I wasn't laughing at you at all. I confess I had insane notions that we would share a night of unbridled sex after what I heard about you at the club. You have the reputation for being a right little raver, but I see now that I was set up. Indeed we both were."

"Oh no!" She glared at him owl-like, her eyes wide with disbelief.

"Oh yes. I suspect your *good friend* Simon Dean had something to do with it."

"Why would he do that?" she cried.

"Who knows. I told you he's an obnoxious individual."

Leonie huddled under the covers

feeling vulnerable and out of her depth. Scott looked so devilishly appealing with his ruffled hair and impish eyes. Eyes that now surveyed her critically, and she lowered her own feeling deeply embarrassed. The whole episode was so unreal — at least it was for her. Jolie would have been highly amused, she was well used to her friends' so called pranks.

Leonie wondered what was going through his head now, and said the first thing that sprang to mind. "I'm allergic to garlic. I don't know what was in the meal we had last night, but I suspect garlic. I'm sorry . . . I hope what has happened . . . I mean what will your fiancée . . . I'm sorry." She stuttered miserably.

4

LEONIE heard him singing in the shower. It was a song she recognised and she smiled ruefully remembering the lyrics. She found herself imagining what he must look like as he soaped himself all over, and blushed when recalling his teasing suggestion that she could scrub his back for him. She couldn't believe what was happening to her. It was if she'd had a brainstorm or a personality transplant. Why was she even now imagining him naked? He wasn't her fiancé or even her boy friend. After her latest revelations she couldn't think he would want to have anything more to do with her.

She was still sitting in bed in a bemused state when he emerged with a towel loosely draped round his waist.

"You look like a wild gypsy with your hair all awry. Trying to tempt me after all?" he inquired with a characteristic lift of an eyebrow. He looked at his watch and sighed. "There isn't time now I'm afraid. You'd best get dressed or we'll be late for our appointment."

She found herself staring again at his impressive physique. She had never been in such close contact with a near naked man before, and the sight of his chest and the way his muscles rippled as he reached into the wardrobe for a clean shirt were enough to make her eyes widen in admiration. Then, realising what he intended doing she quickly made her escape into the bathroom, followed by his cynical laugh. He was obviously well aware of her scrutiny and clearly not at all embarrassed by it.

Leonie sat on the edge of the bath feeling weak and immature. Catching sight of her white face in the mirror, she grimaced. She looked terrible. She wasn't sure whether it was the after effects of the garlic, or the predicament she found herself in with Scott. She was so confused that she wasn't sure what she felt any more.

"See you downstairs in ten minutes," he called banging on the door. "The key's on the dressing table."

After a reviving shower Leonie dressed, brushed her hair and clipped it back with combs, but it appeared to have a will of its own. She scanned her face and saw how desperately pale she looked even with make-up, but since she hadn't brought any blusher there was no more she could do about it. Somehow or other she had to get through another day with Scott.

Dressed in a clean blouse and tailored suit she steeled herself to cope with whatever lay ahead. At least by late evening they would be safely back in Chellow and that would be the end of it she hoped. She went downstairs feeling definitely queasy and not at all interested in breakfast. The smell of bacon cooking was sufficient to make her stomach revolt. They met up in the foyer. He took her by the arm and escorted her into the dining room looking angry and quite formidable.

"You'll be no use to me looking like that. Are you sure you're all right? You look dreadful."

"Thank you for those few kind words," she snapped back at him. "I didn't ask to come on this jaunt. I have work I should be doing at home. Heaven alone knows what Tina is thinking. I've had to leave her to cope with whatever turned up. She can't contact me because you forgot to inform me of our destination, remember?"

"She should be used to it by now, surely?"

"I wish you'd stop your insinuations."

He shrugged his shoulders impassively.

Leonie settled for fruit juice, toast and coffee and then had to sit and watch Scott demolish a full cooked breakfast. She felt slightly better for the food and the colour returned to her cheeks.

Back in the bedroom she managed

to scoop her hair off her face into a more business-like style and hoped it would stay put.

It was only a short ride to Sterne Enterprises — a modern building on the outskirts of the city. They hadn't long to wait before being ushered into the manager's office and were introduced to Giorgio Sterne. He was a charming man with gentle grey eyes, fair hair and an engaging personality. Once the formalities were over Leonie opened her notepad and tried to make herself inconspicuous.

"I believe these brochures will convince you that Andrews Electronics have all the components you need," Scott said unearthing several items from his brief-case. "Andy, my partner promised you the up-to-date ones, didn't he?"

Giorgio nodded. "He seemed to think that your AE123 would be suitable for our purposes. Since I last spoke with him however, we have made some alterations to our product and maybe it isn't quite so suitable now."

The discussion progressed reasonably amicably, and then a tour of the assembly line was suggested, Leonie included. All in all it was a pleasant morning and everything appeared highly satisfactory. They left with the strong impression that Giorgio Sterne would place the order shortly once the financial side was ironed out.

In the car park Scott grinned at Leonie and winked, he seemed to be in excellent spirits. "You bowled him over. He couldn't take his eyes off you. You certainly have quite an effect on the opposite sex for one so innocent."

"Rubbish," she replied although perfectly well aware that Scott's remark was nearer the truth where Giorgio Sterne was concerned at least. "You still didn't get your order, did you?"

"We will. He obviously wants to price out our opposition, that's all."

"And you think you'll beat them — on price and delivery?"

"Of course. Come along, I think that deserves a slap up lunch. We've several hours to kill before our flight. Has your appetite returned?"

She nodded and smiled — a smile of relief.

Scott drove out of the city and soon they were wending their way up a narrow road through splendid scenery to a small mountain village. He pulled into a hotel car park with a flourish, obviously having been before. It was a typical Austrian construction of timber, with many ornate balconies and fancy window shutters. Leonie thought it delightful.

The dining room was not busy and they were straightaway shown to a table with utmost courtesy, and handed impressive menus. Leonie saw hanging on the wall nearby pictures of snow covered mountains, cable cars and gaily coloured skiers, and felt her cheeks flame. This was where Scott came skiing, and she could well understand why. It had the most scintillating scenery and a wonderful freshness. The air felt invigorating cold, but not damp like back home. She would love to have gone for a walk to try to blow away some of the cobwebs from her brain. It was certainly well and truly addled.

"It's beautiful," she said gazing out of the window at the mountains across the valley. "This is where you come skiing?"

"Hmm," he said glancing up from the menu. "Whenever I get the opportunity."

The waiter returned and took their order. Afterwards Scott pursed his lips and frowned. "I can't work you out. How the devil did you get under my skin the way you did? I'm a pretty hard nosed business man most of the time — or so my competitors say. How come I became bewitched by a pair of honey coloured eyes? I don't need that kind of distraction. In fact I can well do without it right now."

Leonie idly played with a bread roll not sure how to respond.

"Have you any idea what effect you have on me I wonder? Maybe it isn't only me though," he went on with a sigh. "I swear Giorgio couldn't take his eyes off you either."

Leonie raised her head marginally and peeked at him through her eyelashes. She mentally pictured how he'd looked that morning when he came from the shower, and it sent her blood racing. If only he knew what effect he was having on her! To retain any sort of equilibrium she had to bear in mind what Simon had told her about Scott, although she was having doubts about the validity. Scott didn't seem the sort of person to be devious. There must be some other explanation, and yet — he hadn't refuted that he was engaged she recalled.

"What gossip did you hear about me?" she asked.

"I inquired around at the club and got a mixed response. Some sang your praises as being a competent business woman with extremely high standards."

"And the others?"

When Scott didn't elaborate she

glared at him. "You really did think that I was one of *those* sort of women, didn't you!" It was written all over his face.

"Well, if you will consort with the likes of Simon Dean," he retorted, "you only have yourself to blame."

"I told you, he is a business acquaintance that's all. He was Jolie's friend not mine. I told you right from the start that I provide secretarial services pure and simple. That is the only involvement I have with Simon. I had never been out with him before that night. I am sorry about your speech," she went on, feeling that it was now time to clear the air, "but I did deliver it as promised, and in plenty of time too, only I did ask them not to give it to you until afterwards. I'm very sorry about that. I was angry because I wrongly blamed you for Jolie's death. I realise that I was at fault and deserved some sort of punishment, so if you decide to tell all your cronies at the club that I am not to be trusted then I can't stop you, but I don't get my business by going to bed with my clients. I draw the line at that."

Scott grinned ruefully at her tirade. "Relax, I guess we both acted rather rashly in the circumstances. Shall we leave it at that? We both wanted to hit back at something or someone."

Leonie half smiled. "I hope that I have in some way helped to repay my debt to you, but that is as far as it goes. I suppose if necessary, I can revert to being a one woman business again if you decide to tell everyone that I slept with you, but it's not just me that would be inconvenienced."

"Leonie, believe me I wouldn't do anything so crude. I can only apologise for my own abnormal behaviour, and put it down to simply being infatuated with you. Something strange happened to me at the Flamingo Club that night which left me completely foxed. I haven't been able to get you out of my mind since, but I'll not make trouble for you. This need go no further, I promise, and I'll see to it that Dean doesn't make trouble for you either. After all nothing happened, did it?"

* * *

It was very late when they arrived back in Chellow and Scott dropped her off at the shop.

"Thank you for your assistance, Leonie," he said soberly. "Once again, I'm sorry for causing you any distress. Send me your bill and I'll see it gets paid pronto."

"Let's just say that we're quits shall we?" she replied quietly, relieving him of her suitcase. "It's been an interesting experience."

He looked into her eyes and his lips twitched. She wondered if he was about to kiss her, but he turned away without doing so much to her regret. She still wanted to know what it would be like, and would have responded if he initiated it.

"I'll let you have a transcript of the

notes I took as soon as possible."

"Thanks, that would be much appreciated. Take care of yourself, Leonie. I'll be in touch when I have need of your *secretarial services.*"

Leonie watched him drive off fully aware of his double meaning and knew that she was going to have a lot of explaining to do the next day.

* * *

Tina greeted her with a cheeky grin the following day. "Good morning, boss. Did you have a satisfactory engagement?"

"Illuminating would be a better word for it," she replied. "How about some coffee while I wade through the post." The sooner she got stuck into some office work the better. As an afterthought she called to Tina before she disappeared. "By the way, if Simon Dean rings in future I'm out. I don't care what you tell him, but I don't want to see him again — ever. Got it?"

"Yes, boss. Gladly. It's about time he was sent packing in my opinion. I'd have done it long ago."

* * *

Leonie resorted to putting the answering machine on after office hours. She didn't like doing it but she didn't want to speak to Simon, or for that matter Scott either. Scott disturbed her conscience. She wasn't used to such a dynamic personality. She kept going over all that had happened, and asked herself often whether she would still have gone if she had known what lay in store. Somehow she knew that she would. She had enjoyed the experience even though for the most part she had been frightened and scared. Once he accepted that she wasn't free with her favours as he'd been led to believe Scott had behaved with remarkable solicitude — in fact the perfect gentleman.

* * *

The next Saturday Leonie spring cleaned the flat from top to bottom. She couldn't settle to office work and yet she couldn't bring herself to go anywhere in case Scott rang. Even if he did she didn't propose answering it, but she wanted to hear his voice. She wanted to think that she meant something to him, but that made her feel guilty when she remembered his girlfriend. Late in the afternoon the doorbell rang and when Leonie went to answer it she found herself confronted by a delivery boy with a large parcel.

"Miss Davis? Sign here please."

Leonie went back upstairs clutching the bulky parcel feeling puzzled yet excited. Instinctively she knew it was from Scott and guessed it was in the way of an apology. She tore away the packaging and couldn't believe her eyes when she unwrapped the most beautiful, cuddly teddy bear. It had a ribbon round its neck and a card attached.

"I hope Bruno will be company for

you in your lonely bed."

Tears sprang up immediately, she could well imagine Scott saying the words full of mockery and wicked amusement. All the same she thought it was a most beautiful present — one of the most thoughtful that she had ever received. There was a PS on the reverse of the card. "You shouldn't have any more bother with S Dean. If you do, let me know."

Leonie immediately went to the telephone and switched off the answering machine. She began dialling Scott's number, but then paused. Perhaps it would be more prudent in the circumstances to write a short note of thanks. She went back to her cleaning but spent the greater part of it composing a thank you letter. Scott Andrews was a remarkably sensitive and thoughtful person of that she had no doubt, despite his arrogant manner at times.

Bruno took up residence at first in Leonie's bedroom, but then he gradually followed her around the flat. When she was sitting watching television he was there too. When she went to her office he sat in the chair facing her. In bed he was a source of comfort when she remembered its donor. He made up in a fashion for the lack of Jolie's company.

* * *

Leonie wondered how many of her clients would desert her when Simon made known his displeasure. She didn't know what Scott had said to Simon, but she never heard from him again for which she was extremely thankful.

During the next two weeks several new clients approached 'Girl Friday', mostly from the Trenton area and all apparently recommended by Scott. Leonie became so busy that she was working long hours, as well as all her usual personnel, just to keep pace with the extra work load.

Despite being busy she thought often

of Scott, wondering how he was coping with his hectic schedule. She knew he was finding work difficult since he hadn't managed to find anyone to replace his partner. She would like to have phoned him, but thought it somehow inappropriate. She knew she should be trying to put him out of her mind, but that was pretty nigh impossible. On the way home from Austria they had talked a lot about business problems of one sort and another, and she had learned a little about his busy life, especially so at present.

One evening she was still hard at work when Scott arrived unexpectedly. It was after office hours when she heard his car drawing up outside. She recognised the distinctive exhaust note and hurriedly saved her work before going to greet him.

"Busy?" he asked with a wry, lopsided grin.

"Thanks to you I'm inundated. Do come in. I wanted to ring you to thank you for your involvement, but I . . . Would you like some coffee?"

"Thanks."

Leonie went into her small kitchenette to put the kettle on. She splashed cold water on her face to cool her incriminating flushed cheeks before returning to the lounge. There she found Scott sitting in the armchair holding Bruno as if he'd been having a serious heart to heart conversation with him.

"Bruno is a great comfort," she admitted with a rueful smile. "It may seem immature and childish, but I talk to him, and even though he doesn't answer back I don't feel quite so alone now. It was an extremely thoughtful present."

"I'm pleased. I hoped you'd like him."

"It did cross my mind that you may have sent him to the wrong address. That maybe he belonged to a nephew or niece."

"No such luck, I'm afraid. I'm uncle

to no-one. I only have one sister, and she's been married four years with no sign of any offspring."

"Did you get your order from Giorgio?" Leonie asked, quickly changing the subject. "I've been wondering."

"That is what I came to see you about. He wants me to go over to discuss terms. He especially asked if you would be accompanying me, so what about it?"

"He probably wants to meet your fiancée, Scott," she said quietly, sadly. "You'll have to straighten him out. I didn't know what to say at the time, and somehow it never did get put right. He just assumed . . . "

Scott frowned, and looked at his shoes in pensive concentration. "Penny isn't a fiancée in the true sense of the word."

Leonie paused in the act of offering him a shortbread biscuit. "How do you mean?"

"It's rather a strange situation I find myself in. Penny was Andrew's sister.

When he died she inherited his share of the company. Penny has always been a bit of a spendthrift, so I guessed that when she got her hands on the shares she would think about selling them, which is precisely what she did. She was immediately approached by a certain individual who shall remain nameless.

"She came and told me about his offer, mistakenly believing that I had first refusal on them. If she had read the paperwork more thoroughly she would have realised that she could sell to whom ever she pleased, and there was nothing I could do about it. Anyway, she still believes that, and I haven't informed her otherwise.

"At the time I wasn't in a position to buy the shares myself, and yet as you may appreciate, I didn't welcome the thought of another partner being imposed on me. Especially this particular guy. How would you feel if someone was inflicted on you like that, and you had no say in the matter? It made my blood boil to think of all that Andy and I had built up could be ruined. The answer lay in persuading Penny to hold on long enough until I was in a position to buy her out. I didn't expect it to take long. I have assets but they weren't easily turned into cash.

"It was Penny's suggestion that we announced our engagement as a way of keeping this chap, or any others from badgering her. It is purely a business transaction, nothing more. I have nothing against Penny, but she wouldn't be my choice for a wife."

"For the moment though, you are still engaged to her?"

"Yes, unfortunately that is so, if one is strictly honest, but I didn't buy her a ring or anything. It wasn't meant to be a permanent solution. Penny's had such a traumatic time recently — you understand. Until she's had more time to get over her grief, I don't feel I can . . . but . . . well, you must know how I feel about — " He left the sentence in mid air.

Leonie's hopes rose. Did he mean what she thought he meant?

"I would really appreciate it if you would come with me. If you like you can put it on a business footing and send me a bill for your time, although I won't need secretarial assistance this trip, merely the pleasure of your company."

Leonie was in two minds about what she should do. Her heart told her that she should go and enjoy herself, but then her conscience told her to be sensible. The thought of seeing Austria again was a great attraction, and almost irresistible. Being with Scott would be a bonus, especially after what he'd just told her.

"I would welcome a chance to get to know you better. No strings attached! Don't I deserve a chance to redeem myself?"

"When did you want to go?" she asked breathlessly.

His face lit up. "I thought if we flew out late Thursday, we could have

Friday to see to the business end of things, and then have a day for sightseeing before flying back on Sunday. Think you can manage that?" His eyes pleaded with her. "The weather forecast is good — mild and sunny, which is unusual for April."

"I'm sorely tempted. I have got rather a lot of work on, but since it was your doing that we have so many new clients I can hardly refuse you can I? By the way, what did you say to Simon? I haven't seen or heard from him since we got back from Austria."

"I put him straight about a few things that's all," he grinned and rubbed his knuckles. "He's a bit of a coward actually. His sort usually are."

* * *

Tina was all agog about the mystery trips but Leonie didn't tell her any more than she needed to know. That only served to incite her still further. Leonie didn't want anyone telling tales about the proposed visit, and also she felt it was something special which she wished to keep to herself. She knew exactly what the people of Chellow would think if they knew, and Tina was such a gossip.

Leonie had been nervously excited ever since she had agreed to go. She knew she wasn't viewing it as a business arrangement as she should, but kept reminding herself of what Jolie would say if she'd been alive. Maybe one could mix business with pleasure occasionally she thought. One should make the most of any opportunity — grasp it with both hands since life could be cut short.

"I'm sorry, Tina this came up unexpectedly. I hope you can cope on your own again." Leonie tried to placate a rather subdued employee as she waited for Scott to arrive on the Thursday afternoon. "If you have any doubts about anything then delay a decision until I get back on Monday, but otherwise you're in charge."

Tina brightened up. "No problem,

boss. I'll be all right here on my own. The extra pay will come in useful too. You deserve a break, so try to enjoy it. I would jump at the chance of a few days away with a heart throb like him!"

"And what about your husband pray? Wouldn't he have something to say about it?"

"I was merely daydreaming," she pouted.

"This is an important business trip which means a lot to Mr Andrews. If all goes according to plan it will mean more work and more employment for his firm. Besides, his recommendations have brought us many more clients, so the least I can do is assist him if I can. Just make sure you keep your mind on your work while I'm away. Don't forget our code of practice, I don't want anyone letting the side down."

"Your chauffeur is pulling up outside," said Tina, rushing to pick up Leonie's suitcase. "Want me to give you a hand?

5

IT was late when they arrived at the hotel, even though they had flown direct to Innsbruck airport this time. It wasn't the same hotel they had stayed at previously, but one in an intriguing little village a few miles out of town. The ride alone through the narrow lanes had been most enjoyable, and being with Scott increased Leonie's pleasure. He'd played his part well in front of Tina, obviously well aware of the effect he was having on her.

Leonie smiled ruefully, when she saw the manager hand Scott two keys and noted Scott's reaction when told that they were next door to each other.

"Sleep well, Leonie." His tone was bland as they parted company outside her room. "Herr Sterne can't accommodate us until after lunch so we have a free morning."

It took Leonie a long, long time getting to sleep knowing that Scott was in the room the other side of the wall. She envisaged him stepping fresh from the shower with his hair rumpled and looking enticingly sexy. For such a big man he was superbly built with little surplus fat. The nickname she'd invented for him suited him perfectly she thought. He was the epitome of her ideal mate, except he was engaged to another, albeit temporarily.

She thumped the pillow and sighed. Could she really believe it when he said his engagement was a phoney, or was that a come-on? Was he saying it in all honesty or simply to encourage her to be available and fall in with his wishes more readily? She needed very little encouragement on that score, but she wished she was more worldly-wise. Why couldn't she have been more like Jolie who had been happy to have various affairs and not taken life so seriously? Maybe she should take a leaf out of her book.

So far she had refrained from getting too deeply involved with anyone, and in her book love was what mattered. Sex for the sake of it wasn't for her — at least that was how she had felt up until now. For the first time in her life she was beginning to have doubts about her high moral stance. She wasn't sure if it was love or lust she felt for Scott, only that she wanted to be with him.

* * *

The next day they spent a pleasant morning strolling round Innsbruck at Scott's suggestion. He was in exceptional humour, seemingly happy to meander about the old streets, in and out of the tourist shops, occasionally trying to persuade her to accept a souvenir.

"You've already given me a present," she reminded him flirtatiously. "I have Bruno."

"That was in way of an apology. This would be different. This would be because I like being with you, and I'd like you to have something that will be a constant reminder of our time here."

"I'll never be able to forget our stay here. I'm enjoying every minute. Just look at those decorated buildings. Aren't they splendid? I wonder how they manage to paint such beautiful pictures like that? It must be awful when they have to redecorate. Fancy having to paint over them. I suppose I should be feeling guilty about being here with you but I don't. I have hardly given my business a thought all morning, although I expect I shall know all about it when I get back."

He squeezed her hand. "One has to make the most of times such as these. I expect, like me that you work longer and harder than anyone else you employ. It's tough being the boss isn't it?"

"True," she agreed, "but I wouldn't have it any other way. I enjoy my work and the achievement of having a healthy bank balance. It makes me feel good too when I provide work for others, and help them financially."

They stopped to look in a shop window and Leonie promptly took a liking to a pair of earrings on display. They were fashioned in the shape of tear-drops and were made of Austrian crystal.

"Let me buy them for you," Scott said.

After several minutes in friendly argument she gave in, she could see that it would please him if she accepted them as a gift. They weren't very expensive but had captured her fancy. Scott insisted that she wore them straightaway and they went for lunch laughing at the way the shopkeeper had tried to interest them in more expensive jewellery.

Scott knew his way around the town, having spent several holidays in the area, and guided her to a restaurant down a side street. It was only small but attractively decorated and fairly quiet.

"Hungry?" he asked.

"Famished. I must admit I normally have a healthy appetite."

"That's what I like to hear. None of this lettuce leaf and mineral water stuff."

"What do you recommend?" she asked with a laugh.

Scott put aside the menus and when the waiter arrived asked for the house speciality.

"I hope there's no garlic in it," she grinned.

"Positive. Do you think I want a repetition of our last visit? Though come to think of it, you were helpless in my arms at the time, and only wearing some frilly lace whatnot. Maybe there is something to be said for it."

Leonie flushed at the memory.

"I missed my chance there didn't I? What should I read into your modest blush, Leonie, I wonder? Has nobody ever captured your heart? I can't believe that you are as chaste as you portray somehow."

"You seem to have overcome my natural reticence," she remarked coyly. "I would never have dared leave home with a complete stranger like I did with you."

"Ah, but I didn't give you much option did I?"

"I could have refused. I do know how to look after myself you know. Jolie and I went to a personal survival group once."

Scott looked amused. "Think you could throw me over your shoulder? I rather like the idea of you trying."

Leonie instantly realised that she was getting into deeper trouble and quickly changed the subject.

* * *

After an extremely enjoyable lunch they made their way to Sterne Enterprises. Leonie felt nervous despite having Scott's assurance that there was nothing to worry about. She had butterflies in her stomach and wished that she could have returned to the hotel. Scott could have made her excuses to Giorgio — plead a headache or something.

The receptionist informed them that Herr Sterne was in a meeting and suggested they took a seat. They waited and waited with Scott getting more and more agitated. Finally, almost half an hour late they were shown into Herr Sterne's office.

He rose to greet them apologising for the delay, but his manner was coldly formal, and not at all like on the previous occasion. He almost scowled in Leonie's direction.

"Is there a problem, Giorgio?" Scott asked. It was evident that something was causing concern.

"I'm not sure," Giorgio said slowly. "It was too late to contact you, but unfortunately I'm not in a position to complete our contract today. Something has come up rather unexpectedly. You are staying overnight I take it?"

"Yes, but at the Alpina in Inton this time," Scott replied with curt, business-like briskness.

"Very nice and discreet. A wise choice," was the subdued response. "Perhaps by tomorrow . . . "

"Have you been offered a better deal elsewhere, may I ask?"

Giorgio nodded. "They say they can undercut your price by five per cent."

"I see," murmured Scott.

"I'm afraid . . . "

"I don't know if I can match that. Let me go over the figures again and see what I can come up with. I might manage two per cent. I presume you are still open to negotiations?"

"But of course."

They were shown out with dignified courtesy, but Leonie was almost totally ignored.

Scott looked grim as they got back into the car. He sat drumming his fingers on the steering wheel for a few minutes staring out at a brick wall. Leonie couldn't think of anything to say that would help so sat in unhappy silence. Finally he snapped on his seat belt and pulled out to join the rush hour traffic. Nothing was said all the way back to their hotel. She knew Scott had taken it as a deliberate snub and wouldn't want to hear her thoughts on the subject.

At the hotel Scott headed for his room muttering about going over the figures refusing any assistance from her. Leonie went to her room and stared out of the window. It was her fault that Scott hadn't got the contract. She just knew it. That being so it was up to her to her to do something about it. Leaving a note for Scott at the reception desk she took a taxi back to Sterne Enterprises. It was worth a try at any rate, and she didn't think she had anything to lose by it.

She had a few minutes to wait before Giorgio was free in which she rehearsed her version of events. She felt nervous but knew that she had to do it.

"Herr Sterne, I appreciate your taking time to see me." Leonie said in hesitant German. She felt it may help her cause if she spoke in his own language, albeit not very fluently.

"You speak German, Leonie? I didn't realise." His manner was cool but courteous.

"A little," she replied and then continued in English. "I can translate fairly well but I'm not very good at conversation."

"You are a rather unusual young lady. I somehow rather expected you to return." He half smiled as if relenting. "Please take a seat. I can guess why you've come."

Leonie immediately launched into her prepared speech. "I believe you've had some correspondence from Simon Dean. Is he the person who has offered you a better deal?"

Giorgio slowly nodded.

"I thought so. I can also guess what he inferred. Herr Sterne, Scott and I are friends — business acquaintances that is all, I do assure you. Scott was misled the same as you about the kind of service I provide. I run a secretarial agency not an escort service."

Giorgio smiled, relaxed back in his chair and inclined his head urging her to continue.

"Simon Dean is a property developer amongst other things. I don't suppose for an instant that he could sell you the chips you need, or at least if he can, he wouldn't be able to provide the continuity that Scott can. I suspect he is angry because he tried to buy into Scott's company when Andrew died and Scott wouldn't have anything to do with him."

"What makes you sure?"

"Simon told me so himself. Simon has put business my way but when I learned what a dishonourable person he was I refused to have anything more to do with him. He is obviously trying to get back at both of us. I just thought you ought to be aware of what sort of person you are dealing with. Scott doesn't know I've come, this was my own idea. I didn't want Scott to lose business on account of me. He's been having a tough time recently with the loss of his partner."

Leonie got to her feet. "I'd better go . . . "

Giorgio also rose and walked round the desk. "I wonder, Leonie if you would care to have dinner with me? I'd like to hear more. Is it true that Scott is engaged to Andrew's sister?"

"Yes," she said. What else could she say.

"I had every intention of signing up with Andrews Electronics you know," Giorgio chuckled as he escorted her from his office "but I thought it was an excellent lever to get a better deal. I've been trying unsuccessfully all morning to learn something about Simon Dean. As you so rightly point out I need a good source of supply with reliable continuity, so I won't deal with a fly by night operator. In the circumstances though the opportunity to enjoy your charming company I feel should not be lost."

"I'll never understand business ethics,"

sighed Leonie. "My friend Jolie always said I ought to toughen up."

* * *

Leonie spent the evening with Giorgio. He was perfectly charming. They went to a cosy restaurant in the centre of Innsbruck where he was obviously well known. The owner welcomed him like an old and valued friend.

"Fritz has known my family since I was so high," Giorgio said, smilingly demonstrating with his hand three feet off the ground.

"I'm not taking you away from your family tonight am I?" Leonie asked.

"I'm not married, Leonie — not even a girl friend at the moment. I meant my parents and brothers. We all have Fritz to thank for his discerning thoughts on just about any topic you care to mention, along of course with his gastronomic feasts. Whenever I have important clients to entertain I bring them here. Not only do we get gourmet food but expert advice as well. Is that not so, Fritz?"

Giorgio was a true gentleman and Leonie enjoyed his company. She told him about her business and what she knew about Scott. He in turn was a mine of information about the local beauty spots, and made many suggestions of what she ought to see in so short a visit. When he dropped her off at the hotel later he handed her the signed paperwork for Scott.

"I would like to be counted as your friend, Leonie, and I see trouble ahead if you continue down your present track. Take care, and remember, I would be delighted to have you come and work for me anytime."

"Thank you, Giorgio. I appreciate your understanding in this matter. I'll bear it in mind because one never knows what may happen in these days of recession. I would have to brush up on my German though, it's very rusty at present."

Leonie entered the hotel intent on

slipping the signed document under Scott's door, but as she made her way to reception to collect her key he strode out of the bar where he'd been lying in wait for her.

"Where the devil have you been?" he growled bleakly. "I've been looking all over for you."

"Having dinner," she replied calmly and politely. "I didn't think you were in any mood for my company this evening."

"What gave you the temerity to decide what I thought."

She handed him the envelope which Giorgio had given her.

"What's this?"

"Read it and it might explain a few things. Good-night, Scott." She hurried into the lift just as the doors closed leaving him tearing open the envelope with a bewildered look on his face. She wasn't surprised when he knocked on her door a few minutes later.

"How did you get this?" he asked incredulously.

"Well, I didn't sleep with him if that is what you're thinking. I simply told him the truth. You may not have noticed, but I did. On his desk this morning was some correspondence from Simon Dean. I recognised the distinctive stationery, so I put two and two together."

"Why the devil didn't you tell me? I've been wracking my brains wondering who the competitor could be."

"You weren't exactly approachable after the meeting were you?"

"You've been with Giorgio all this time?"

"He took me out to dinner and told me that he was only trying to screw the price down, but he intended giving you the contract anyway."

"Leonie, I could kiss you. I'm sorry for being so touchy. I've had a lot on my plate recently. I can't afford to lose this contract. It means a great deal."

The pleasant evening with Giorgio had relaxed her. Lulled by the wine they'd had at dinner she looked up at him smiling intimately, thinking dreamy thoughts, and her lips parted invitingly. In an instant she was enveloped in his arms and with great tenderness his lips devoured hers. The kiss began soft as thistledown, but soon they were fervently demanding, nibbling and probing.

It was as wonderful, if not more so than she had ever imagined, and she wound her hands round his neck so he couldn't escape. Their bodies melded together and she could feel his hard arousal as his hands gently manipulated her hips against him. There was instant conflagration between them which she couldn't disguise. Instead of backing away at the seduction, she was encouraging him, welcoming the feel of his firm muscular body.

Sensing her approval he set about disrobing her, his hands gliding up under her blouse to unclasp her bra. They found their target and she gasped with pleasure at the sensuously light touch of his fingers brushing her overheated skin. Her heart was pounding and she could feel herself spiralling out of control. She knew she was crazy for feeling the way she did about him, and it would be far better to fall for someone like Giorgio, but that wasn't how it worked. Her heart had a will of its own. It was telling her that she loved him and that made it all right.

For a split second she wondered, did he think she was easy prey for a casual fling, or was it something more meaningful he had in mind? Was this a purely one sided affair? She found her answer in his eyes. They melted her resolve and she offered him her lips again, revelling in his invasion of her senses.

"Oh Leonie," he whispered. "I do want you. Heaven alone knows why, but I'm behaving like an adolescent schoolboy. I've never felt like this before. Being with you is like a dream come true."

She gulped and tried to push him away. Steeling herself she said quietly. "I think you'd better go. It's been a long day and I'm tired."

She heard and felt him heave as she buried her head on his chest. She wasn't putting up much of a struggle, and he gently removed his hands and straightened her blouse.

"Is that what you truly want?" he whispered his voice ragged and strained.

She sobbed and clung to him trying to deny her desire for him, but it was no use. She wanted him like she'd never wanted any man before in her life, and it was quite a shock to find how undisciplined her body had become.

He began removing the clips from her hair letting it cascade down her back, and rifling his hands though it he massaged her neck turning her bones to liquid.

"Are you really sending me away to my cold, lonely bed, Leonie?

Wouldn't you like me to take Bruno's place tonight?" he pleaded. "You look wonderfully wild and sexy with your hair free and unrestrained — tantalisingly erotic. I want you so badly. I've never felt so disturbed as I do right now, but I'll go if that is what you truly want. I'll probably have to spend the rest of the night having cold showers, and it will serve me right I know."

His kisses were doing untold damage until she was powerless to resist any more. His voice so persuasive and tender, his hands again exploring her body sparking off pure wanton desire. She felt complete abandonment. This was what she had yearned for, ever since their first meeting at the Flamingo Club. He knew it and she knew it. She was literally trembling with desire to know Scott more intimately. For the first time in her life she was being audacious. She was deliberately flaunting herself and enjoying the sensuousness of it.

* * *

The next morning she woke to find Scott had returned to his own room which she felt was rather diplomatic in view of what had happened. She rolled over, hugged the pillow and smiled happily. He loved her and she loved him, that much was patently obvious. She wasn't sure where it would lead, if anywhere, but for the moment she didn't care.

It was a beautiful, beautiful day and she was going to spend it with Scott. She bounced out of bed and flung back the curtains, debating what to wear for such an auspicious occasion. She had experienced the most sensational night of her entire life so whatever happened in the future she would always have that to dream about. She was a woman — a woman in love and Scott loved her.

She chose to wear slacks that she had packed at the last moment since they were probably going to do some sight-seeing, and they seemed the most sensible choice. A sunshine yellow jumper and the scarf which had brought Scott to her door in the first place completed the outfit.

Scott looked devastating. She observed him across the breakfast table and thought it unfair that any man could be so attractive casually dressed as he was in pale blue T-shirt and jeans. She thought the informal clothes made him appear younger and more boyish and definitely heart stopping. For an instant she felt gauche and shy when they met wondering if he had any regrets. It appeared not. He was looking at her with great tenderness as if he couldn't believe his luck.

They both left their rooms at the same time and met in the corridor. He'd smiled and intimately put his arm around her waist as they walked down to breakfast. It felt so natural — so familiar. Leonie was on cloud nine.

"Have you any suggestions on what we do today?" he asked passing her the milk for her cornflakes.

A mental picture of how it would be if they were married skipped into her mind. She blinked at the thought of what she'd really like to do but said candidly that she had. "I promised Giorgio . . . "

"You're not deserting me today," he exploded.

"If you'll let me finish," she said, quietly amused. "He recommended that we visit a small village a few miles away."

"Sorry." He grinned ruefully. "I like Giorgio but I don't want to share you with him — not today of all days."

"It's a beautiful country what I've seen of it. Giorgio told me a little about the area and offered himself as guide," she teased. "I regretfully declined though. Didn't you say that you came here skiing? You must know the district then."

"Hmm. That is why I tried very hard to get business in this region. It gives me a good excuse to return.

In the summer it's ideal for walking holidays, and as you know in winter it's a skiers' paradise. Since you are new to the district you'll have to place yourself in my hands and I will be your tour guide for the day."

"Sounds promising," she replied happily. She didn't really mind where they went as long as they were together.

* * *

"I never realised that women could be quite so devious," Scott reflected lying stretched out on the grass with his hands behind his head. It was late afternoon after a splendid day sight-seeing. Leonie had never seen such fantastic scenery. Scott was an interesting guide, pointing out the peaks and naming quite a few of them, even though his attention was primarily focused on the road.

They had motored into the mountains in the morning and explored pretty alpine villages, then lunched at a pleasant cafe overlooking one of the many breathtaking valleys. After lunch they set off to walk up a wooded hillside to a place of renowned scenic beauty which Scott knew about. He showed her where he went skiing and joked about teaching her to ski sometime.

To Leonie it was a crazy, wonderful day. For once in her life she was doing something which she felt in her bones was wrong but didn't feel guilty. How could one feel guilty when one was enjoying oneself so much? The weather was simply glorious, and on their way back to the car they came across a shady glade just off the track. It was so idyllic that it was inevitable that they stopped. Neither of them wanting the day to end.

Leonie turned on to her stomach and looked at him sternly. "I take exception to that remark. I believe in telling the truth as far as possible at all times."

"I wasn't meaning you, Leonie. I was thinking about Penny."

Leonie sighed, sat up and hugged her knees. The mention of Penny was enough to spoil the mood. She had managed to keep all thoughts of Scott's fiancée at bay for most of the day, but now they came flooding back to damage her fragile acceptance that after today she may never see him again.

Scott draped his arm around her shoulders and ran his fingers through her hair twisting it playfully. "Having got to the ripe old age of thirty-four without finding a woman that I wanted to live with for the rest of my life, I began to think that none existed. When Penny told me how Dean was trying to muscle in on her shares and made the suggestion that we became engaged, I couldn't see any harm in it. It was meant to be a stop gap that's all, but now she's wanting to go the whole hog, and for us to get married.

"I don't know why she's suddenly started putting me under such pressure," he said sitting up with a brooding look on his face. "It wasn't what we agreed.

I never had any intention of actually marrying her. I've always enjoyed my freedom too much and she knew that. Now that I've met you I know that there's no way I can be happy with her or anyone else. It's you I've been waiting to meet all this time. Why couldn't we have met six months ago before catastrophe struck, sweetheart?"

Leonie leaned against him welcoming his embrace. The day had been such fun. Scott had shown his affection in so many ways that she was totally convinced that he felt the same as she did, and yet — Life was unfair. It was the tale of her life, if only, if only . . .

"I think it would be best if we didn't meet again," she said quietly, staring up between the pine trees at the clear blue sky. "At least . . . Until you've resolved this thing with Penny."

"Please don't shut me out of your life, Leonie. I need you. I promise you that I'll work something out. Andy was a good mate of mine so obviously I don't want to cause Penny more trouble; she's been through a lot recently, but soon . . . "

"Don't make promises that you can't fulfil, Scott. Let's make the most of the time we have today, here in this enchanting countryside. I don't want to think about home or Penny and other problems. To me this is a fantasy. I know it and you know it." She turned to look at him. "You know that Giorgio offered me a job, and I might even take him up on it. I couldn't think of a nicer place to work."

"You can't, I won't let you. Besides, what about your business? Are you prepared to give it all up just like that?"

"One day I may have to," she said simply. The thought of being so close and yet not able to meet might become too much to contend with. What if Penny had her way and somehow persuaded Scott to marry her? That would make living in Chellow totally unacceptable Leonie thought miserably.

It was much too close to Trenton for comfort. She shouldn't have become involved with him until he was free. She should have put up more resistance.

"How do you mean? I thought trade was picking up and that you were snowed under with work."

"For the moment I am, but it fluctuates quite a bit, and if for any reason my reputation in Chellow became tarnished it could all disappear overnight. The people of Chellow are more parochial than Trenton and have high moral standards as you know. I'm still worried about what Simon might do. I don't think we've heard the last of him."

"Let me worry about him. If he causes you any trouble, tell me. I can't say I'm too happy about the sort of people you must encounter in your line of business. I hope they're not all like Dean."

He suddenly had an inspiration, she saw his eyes glint with excitement. "I say, why don't you come and work for me? You could be my personal assistant. That would be marvellous don't you think? What could be better now that I have to get out meeting clients more? We could travel the world together. Wouldn't that be wonderful mixing business with pleasure, and you've proved what an asset you are. The way you handled Giorgio was masterful. What do you say?"

"That's not the answer, Scott. It wouldn't work. You know how I feel. I'll deal with Simon in my own way if he causes any more trouble. I'm used to standing on my own two feet. I have to since I have no-one since . . . "

"Please, Leonie. You have me now."

"No, I haven't." Her eyes filled and she looked away. "I can't believe this is happening to me. I can't believe I'm behaving like this. It's not like me at all."

Suddenly the whole episode was turning sour. The thought of going home and back to reality was most depressing.

"How come you were brought up in a children's home? I've never met anyone who had no relatives before."

"Both my parents died when I was nine years old and I gather there was no close relative to take charge of me."

"How very sad. It must have been a traumatic experience, and yet you are remarkably self sufficient for one so young. Maybe you do have relatives that you don't know about. Would you like me to . . . "

"Please, Scott. We'd better go. I shouldn't have come. I knew what would happen. We're just making matters worse." She didn't want to talk about relations and relationships. It was something she always tried to avoid.

He took her by the shoulders, pushing her gently down on to the grass. Caressingly he pushed the hair off her forehead and smoothed away the furrows lining it. "I love you, my sweet. I can't stop touching you, holding you, kissing you. I like to see a smile on your face. I like to hear you laugh. I love stroking your gorgeous hair. I want you beside me however it can be achieved. Believe me, Leonie, I'll do whatever it takes."

She surrendered again to his invading, tantalising lips, promising herself that this was for the last time. It was such heavenly torture that she couldn't resist.

6

"THIS isn't the way back to Chellow." Leonie smiled in puzzlement.

"No, my love. I'm spiriting you away to my lair so that you can come and admire my etchings. It is Sunday after all. I don't want to take you home until I really must."

"But . . . "

"But me no buts. You don't mind do you?"

"Well . . . no, I suppose not. But we shouldn't be seen together should we? I mean what if . . . ?"

"Leonie, you wouldn't leave me when we could spend a few more precious hours together would you? I promise I'll take you home whenever you say, but first I'd like you to see my flat before it's sold. I'll bet you're dying to see where I seduce the myriad of women you seem to think I've had tucked away in my murky past."

She laughed. "What will you do when you have to move out?"

He grinned. "Would you believe I'm moving in with mother?"

Seeing her look of disbelief he elaborated. "It's not as bad as it sounds actually. I'm moving back into my bachelor pad in the old family home. When I left University I couldn't afford a place of my own, but didn't relish returning to the nest so I turned a room over the garage into my den of iniquity." He leered. "I shan't be able to get up to any mischief with mother's eagle eyes watching my every move. Does that satisfy you?"

Leonie giggled. "What sort of mischief had you in mind?" She loved the light-hearted teasing tone. She couldn't imagine anyone stopping him from doing anything he wanted to do.

"Wait and see," he winked mischievously.

Leonie settled back with delight. She

wasn't in any hurry to go home — back to her lonely flat and the work piled up waiting for her. She accepted that they wouldn't be able to see each other for a while — not until Scott untangled himself from Penny's clutches. He was right too, she had been inquisitive about his flat. She had looked up his address in the telephone book, but since she didn't know Trenton very well it didn't provide much of a clue as to the sort of place it was.

She watched with a sense of pride his tanned forearms as he manipulated the car so effortlessly towards Trenton and thought how truly sexy he was. He'd taken off his jacket at the earliest possible moment and rolled up his sleeves in relaxed, casual fashion stating that he felt more at home out of his conventional suit. She wasn't sure what meaning to place on his remark and settled for smothering a chuckle which gave her a quick smirk.

On the outskirts of Trenton he drew up outside an older type detached house set back off the road, and shielded by a ubiquitous privet hedge. There was a small lawned area on either side of the driveway edged with flowerbeds. He pulled up with a flourish in one of the two marked out parking places. Leonie got out of the car and stood looking up at the ivy clad façade, trying to discover how many flats there were. She guessed three and decided the middle one with the balcony was probably the nicest.

"Here we are," Scott said collecting his case from the boot. "Come on. It's been hours since I've been able to hold you in my arms and tell you precisely what you are doing to my manhood. If you don't want to shock the neighbours we had better . . . "

Leonie hastily made her way to the front door, blushing with embarrassment as his eyes were clearly undressing her where she stood. It was incredible the way he made her feel — so totally uninhibited. Jolie would never have recognised her old friend because Leonie didn't even recognise herself.

They hardly got inside the door of his flat before he was smothering her with kisses and inching the zip of her dress down her back.

"Oh, Leonie, Leonie," he whispered urgently as he pushed the dress from her shoulders letting it fall in a heap at her feet.

She felt the same way too and started to undo his shirt with nervous fingers that seemed to be all thumbs. She didn't recall how they came to be in his bedroom. It was still broad daylight and the sun streamed in the large floor length windows lighting up the focal point of the room with utmost clarity. The bed looked huge and yet in keeping with the spacious room — what little she saw of it. She only had eyes for Scott. She suspected they were in the room with the balcony outside, but Scott wasn't in a hurry to show her round his flat — he had other things on his mind.

"In my dreams you have inhabited my bed for long enough, but now I shall be able to smell your scent on my pillows and know how it feels to have my sexy gypsy making love with me."

They tumbled on to the bed just as the phone rang. There was an extension on the bedside table which blared noisily — insistently. It was a most unwelcome intrusion. He growled impatiently. "Let the damn machine answer it," he muttered pulling her into his arms, but it had broken the magical spell. The sound of the phone reminded Leonie immediately of work. They had left the door open and she could hear the muffled chit-chat as the machine engaged and she gathered the caller was Penny. That brought her down to earth with a bump. She struggled to sit up.

"I'd better go," she said somewhat sadly. "I shouldn't have come."

"Why?" he grumbled trying to haul her under the covers.

She gulped. "You belong to her," she said pointing to the photograph at the side of the bed. It was the first thing she saw when the phone rang. It was as if she was being reproached for acting in such a foolhardy manner. As if Penny was literally there in the room with them accusing them of deceit. She felt cheap and dishonest. She scrambled out of bed and went in search of her clothes feeling ashamed and embarrassed. It was as if someone had thrown a bucket of cold water over her and she was seeing things clearly for the first time.

How they came to be arguing she wasn't sure. She got dressed and asked to be taken home. "Or shall I call a taxi? Maybe that would be best in the circumstances."

He sighed and began pulling on his trousers. "I'll drive you if you insist."

"Please," she said. She was sad at the way it had ended up, but it wasn't her fault.

They parted company outside her shop having partially recovered some composure — sufficient to have a parting kiss at any rate, but it lacked sincerity.

"I'll see you when I get back," he said. "I'm off on Tuesday on another confounded business trip. Penny keeps coming up with them."

"Have a nice time," she said blinking back tears of frustration. She turned and entered her front door feeling thoroughly miserable.

* * *

The abrupt way her business collapsed was quite unbelievable. Before she went away Leonie had been congratulating herself on how many new clients she had on the books, but now it seemed they could manage perfectly well without 'Girl Friday's' assistance. At first she suspected a rival agency of having set up in the area which she wasn't aware of. Maybe even one of her own employees being enterprising, but for all she ferreted around she found out nothing untoward. Even Tina who was usually a good source of information seemed foxed by the loss of so many valued customers.

"What's the matter with everyone?" Tina said belligerently. "Have we become contagious all of a sudden? Anyone would think we had the plague."

Leonie gathered together her paperwork and snapped shut the briefcase with a sigh. "I'm not sure what the problem is but if we go on like this I'm going to have to close down. I can't keep going with so few clients. It's quite unbelievable how so many whom I have dealt with for years and I thought of as friends have suddenly become unavailable."

"They all say the same thing when I do get through," said Tina. "They've either taken someone on full time recently or are coping in house. It is too much of a coincidence to be credible."

"I know, but I haven't time to dwell on it now. I'll have to get my skates on or I'm going to be late. See you later."

Leonie went out to her car still in thoughtful mood. Since returning from Austria she hadn't seen anything of Scott. She knew that he was going to be frantically busy, he had told her so, but she missed him dreadfully all the same. He'd told her that he had to raise some money to buy up Penny's shares and only then when he was in a position to do so could he break off their phoncy engagement. Until such time he was being circumspect — that made sense, but she wished they'd parted on better terms.

Leonie would like to have had his thoughts on what was happening to her business and what she should do about it, but she couldn't bring herself to ring him. If Penny answered she wouldn't know what to say, it was all so awkward. She drove to Clarks in her old but reliable Mini and was welcomed by Roy Clark the managing director whom she had known for many years. He at least greeted her cheerfully as if more than welcome, but unfortunately he appeared to be in a hurry.

"Today it's mundane paperwork so I didn't expect the boss herself."

Leonie grinned. "I'm keeping my hand in. One of my girls couldn't make it so I decided to come myself for a change. Are you satisfied with the service you receive from 'Girl Friday', Roy? Any complaints?"

"No," he replied busily rummaging amongst a heap of paperwork for something he'd lost. "I've no complaints. Some girls are better than others obviously, but you already know that I'm sure."

He finally found what he was looking for and reached for his jacket prior to leaving.

"How's business?" Leonie asked. "You sounded worried last time I was here. Is the work picking up?"

He pulled a face. "We're struggling a bit at the moment, but we are managing to keep our heads above water — just. The bank manager hasn't complained yet anyway. I'll leave you the books in case you have time to bring them up to date shall I?" Roy deposited a bundle of files in front of her. "You know where everything is. I have to go out, but if there is anything else you need ask my foreman will you?"

Leonie began work. Clarks was only a small engineering firm which she had been at pains to encourage. It was run on a shoestring and couldn't afford to keep a full time secretary, especially as she would spend a greater part of her time twiddling her thumbs since there wasn't enough work to keep her occupied. Leonie did the bookkeeping for them which saved them accountancy fees, and once or twice a week one of her work force would go and tidy up the office, file the paperwork and do any necessary typing. By one-thirty Leonie was preparing to leave for her next appointment. She had hoped to talk to Roy further to see if he'd heard any rumours about 'Girl Friday' but unfortunately he still hadn't returned.

As she left Clarks Leonie considered again the possibility that it was Simon Dean that was behind her problems. Was he still spreading mischievous gossip? He'd tried to cause trouble with Giorgio hadn't he? He seemed to be the obvious root of her difficulties, but she didn't know how. It wasn't as if it was just the Chellow clients, but the Trenton ones too that had deserted her. That was what puzzled her most.

She drove to the outskirts of Chellow and pulled into the Chase Hotel car park. The Chase was Chellow's newest hotel, only recently opened and seemed to be doing brisk business by the look of things she noticed. The car park was fairly full, mostly with large opulent vehicles making her modest Mini rather conspicuous, not that she cared. The car was economical and reliable and that was what mattered as far as she was concerned.

She managed to squeeze it in a slot near the entrance which pleased her. Then, patting her hair into reasonable order Leonie collected her bag and brief case and entered the hotel lobby. She must remember to see if the manager would be interested in 'Girl Friday' services she thought glancing round at the exotic decor.

"I have an appointment with Mr Jones," she told the smartly dressed receptionist.

"Room 102, first floor." All very efficient, very courteous.

"I'm sorry," said Leonie, "but would you mind ringing him and say that I'm in reception. I'm Miss Davis from 'Girl Friday'."

Leonie walked over to an alcove and peered out of the window to await the client. She had learned long ago never to visit clients in hotel bedrooms no matter what the excuse. She was miles away thinking about Scott and Austria when she felt a hand in the middle of her back. She twirled round and stared into the amused face of Simon Dean.

"Oh," she gasped taken completely by surprise. "You made me jump."

"Waiting for someone?"

"I'm . . . I'm meeting a client," she replied looking at her watch and frowning.

"Mr Jones?" he asked archly.

"How did you know that?"

He laughed cynically. "My dear Leonie you won't need your notepad and pencil for Mr Jones. His requirements are something much more . . . how shall we put it . . . "

Leonie's cheeks flamed when she grasped what he was leading up to.

"You mean you deliberately got me to come here on a wild goose chase! Mr Dean I have better things to do with my time. I can't afford to waste it."

"Who said it would be a waste? I'm sure we could think of some amusing things to do which I'd be more than willing to pay for," he chortled.

Leonie gritted her teeth and glared at him.

"I don't know what your game is but I'll have no part of it. I am not one of your call girls or whatever they call them. I run a respectable secretarial agency, and if you don't stop bothering me I'll . . . I'll . . . "

"What will you do, Leonie? Call your benefactor Scott Andrews?" He looked smug and self satisfied. "He doesn't frighten me. He's through there if you want to call him. Having a birthday lunch with his fiancée I believe."

"I stand on my own two feet," she snapped keeping her voice as low as possible so as not to draw attention to herself. "You are behind the trouble I've been having aren't you?"

"Trouble?" he queried. "I thought business was booming. Enough for you to take time off to gallivant about the continent on holiday — or was that business too?"

Leonie turned on her heel and marched out of the hotel her face red with anger. She didn't know what he knew but she felt guilty and hurt.

It seemed as if everything was falling about her ears. It had been one thing after another. She would love to have gone to seek solace in Scott's arms, but the sight of him smiling across the table at a woman whom she took to be Penny made her feel almost insanely jealous. He didn't look to be finding it a chore, dining out with his partner's sister!

* * *

"Why do I bother?" she said sadly to herself that evening. "It doesn't seem worth the effort. Jolene was correct, I haven't got the right attitude. I'm not tough enough."

The thought of Jolie reminded her of where it had all started — with her wanting revenge, and what a mess she'd made of that! She hugged a cushion and thought about Scott. Had he told Penny that he wanted his freedom? She rather doubted it from what she had seen that afternoon. Once he'd got his order from Giorgio he no longer need her — she had been used, and he was probably even now laughing at her gullibility. He probably never had any intention of buying Penny's shares. What was she to believe? He'd sounded so sincere in Austria. She really believed his promises.

Leonie threw the cushion down and began pacing the floor. She wished she had never met Scott Andrews. Ever since that fateful night at the Flamingo Club she had behaved completely out of character and look where it had got her! Her business was on the rocks, she felt depressed and lethargic and to crown it all she had shared a bed with a man and that was something she had vowed never to do before marriage. She had seen the way Jolie's friends behaved and been let down, and smugly thought it would never happen to her! How wrong could she be!

* * *

By the end of the week the lack of work became intolerable. Finally she succumbed to a particularly nasty dose of 'flu.

"I never get colds," she snuffled angrily. "Why should I get one now — in summer of all times! Nobody gets 'flu in June."

"Off you go and leave everything to me," said Tina full of commiseration. "It is Friday after all. Take the phone off the hook and try to sleep. You need a tonic, that's what you need."

"Maybe a day in bed will revitalise me," Leonie conceded woefully. In the end she spent all Friday and Saturday in bed feeling extremely lethargic and sorry for herself. By Sunday she had made up her mind that it was time to call it a day. After two whole days of thinking and worrying she decided running the business wasn't worth the hassle.

* * *

She drove to Trenton late the following night and parked a little way away from Scott's flat. She wasn't sure if he still owned it, but it was the only place she knew she could see him that was relatively safe from scandal. She felt she just had to see him in the circumstances. She needed to talk to someone. Cautiously she approached the front door watching out for inquisitive neighbours but saw none. Nervously she walked up the stairs to his flat. She thought she heard music coming from inside so was reasonably confident that he was at home — she only hoped that he was alone. She hesitated, reluctant to ring the bell, wondering what his reaction would be.

The door opened unexpectedly quickly and she came face to face with Penny Scot. For a moment neither spoke. Leonie was so overcome with shock that the colour drained from her face. The sight of Scott's fiancée in *his* flat wearing *his* dressing gown was too much.

"Hello. And what can we do for you, Miss Davis?" Penny Scot's tone was scathingly scornful.

"I . . . I . . . I came to see . . . to give this to Scott," Leonie stammered. She had written a note for him just in case he wasn't there, but the last thing she wanted was for him to read it in company. She almost dropped the envelope in her highly-strung state and before she knew what was happening Penny had snatched it from her and was closing the door again. Her parting shot being "I'll give it to him when he gets out of the shower."

Leonie turned and rushed blindly down the stairs. She ran to her car as if the devil was chasing after her. She was mortified. Scott had led her to believe that they didn't have that sort of relationship. He'd said that his connection with Penny were purely platonic and she had truly believed him. She really should have her head examined for behaving so irresponsibly.

* * *

Two days later Leonie gleaned some more disturbing information. Firstly from Roy Clark and then more surprisingly from Simon Dean. It galvanised her into action to speed up her escape from Chellow and all its memories. She couldn't leave soon enough.

Roy rang very early that morning sounding very apologetic and upset. "Leonie, I've just opened the post and . . . and well . . . I'm afraid I'm in trouble."

"I am sorry, Roy. Can I help?" was her immediate response despite her own problems.

There was a long pause before Roy spoke. "I'm afraid I've had a communication from Andrews Electronics. You know I've done quite a bit of work there recently, but now they say that if I continue to use your agency then I'll get no more from them. It's blackmail, pure and simple," he groaned.

"Oh no." Leonie bit back a sob

of disbelief. It was now quite clear what was happening. She'd had her suspicions but now she had definite proof.

"It's all right, Roy," she said quietly. "I was going to ring you to say that I'm closing the business down anyway. The lease is up for renewal and I've decided not to bother. You are the first to know, but I'd appreciate it if you didn't mention it to anyone else at present. I don't want it spread around just yet."

"I'm sorry to hear that but I guess I understand. Business is tough at the moment."

"Thanks for letting me in on what's been happening, Roy. Suddenly I've become almost an outcast and I wondered why. It's all quite clear to me now."

"If there is anything I can do . . . "

"Thanks," she replied. Stifling a sob of misery she put the phone down. It took several minutes to get her temper under control, but then she went in search of Tina.

"I'm truly sorry, Tina, but enough's enough. I can't go on like this. I'm going to have to close down. Now we've lost the Clarks account."

"I'm angry at the way you've been treated." Tina voiced her disapproval in no uncertain terms. "After all the effort you've put in I can't believe it's all for nothing. How can the people of Chellow be so short sighted and vindictive? What have you done to deserve such treatment, I ask you?" Finally she ran out of steam. "Don't worry about me though. Don thinks it is about time I stopped work and started a family, before he gets too old to play with trains. What will you do though? Will you stay in Chellow? Look for other employment?"

"No," said Leonie sadly. "I'm packing up and moving on to pastures new. I can't stay here. Who would employ me anyway? I only hope I can sell up without going bankrupt. That would be all I need."

* * *

Later that very same day Leonie had a surprise visitor. Returning from some late night shopping, it was raining and she didn't take any notice of the car parked outside her shop thinking it most unlikely that it was anyone calling to see her. The first she knew that Simon Dean was waiting was when he relieved her of the shopping. She was balancing it rather awkwardly on one knee as she delved into each pocket for the elusive keys. He'd taken the carrier bags before she realised what he was doing.

"I've come to apologise," was his opening remark. "I'd like to make amends. I've heard about your recent trouble."

"Trouble!" she snapped. "Trouble must be my middle name. Come to gloat have you? Why don't you just leave me alone. You've done enough damage already haven't you?"

The bottom fell out of the remaining

bag she was holding spilling its contents over the pavement. That was the last straw, she was close to tears. Simon helped pick up the tins while she unlocked the door. Afterwards she still didn't know why she had allowed him in. The last time she'd seen him she'd threatened him with the police if he didn't stop bothering her.

"Thanks," she sighed wearily as he deposited everything on the draining board. She felt exhausted and past caring what happened anymore. Scott's betrayal was too much to bear. Nothing mattered.

"You looked bushed. Why don't you go and sit down and I'll make you a nice cup of tea?" Simon said gently.

Leonie shook her head in amazement. This was a side of Simon that she hadn't seen before — one she hadn't expected existed.

"I've come with a proposition for you. Will you hear me out? I promise I'll go whenever you say and no funny business. This time I do sincerely want to help you."

Leonie lethargically nodded her acceptance, and while she put away the groceries he put the kettle on. Then they repaired to the sitting room with the tray of crockery. Leonie was bemused by the change in him. He was almost likeable. She poured the tea and offered him a biscuit, glad of his company in some strange way. It brought back the time not so long ago when he had comforted her after the funeral. He'd been so kind then.

"First, as I said, I want to apologise."

"Giorgio didn't . . . "

"Not the letter to Sterne. I wrote that in a fit of pique. No, I meant because it was me that told Penny Scot about your father. I'm truly sorry in view of what's happened. I guess you've heard that she and Andrews are getting married?"

"You . . . you told her about my father!" Leonie cried clasping her hands to her face. "Oh, no! Why did you do it?" After a pause she added "I presume Jolie told you. She had no right . . . "

He nodded. "She showed me the newspaper cutting in a moment of weakness — don't blame her. She thought it might help me understand you better. She knew that I fancied you, but you always gave me the cold shoulder. She only did it because she was your friend and wanted to help.

"Anyway, as I said, unfortunately I told Penny about your family history when she asked me. At the time I had no idea why she wanted to know, I just thought she was taking a personal interest — because of your involvement with Andrews. I am very sorry, but I never thought she would be so vindictive towards you."

"What was the proposition you have to offer me?" Leonie asked dispassionately. The week which had started out badly she felt couldn't possibly get any worse. All that was left was for her to leave Chellow with as much dignity as possible as quickly as possible.

"I truly wanted you to succeed, Leonie. I did my best to put business your way you know, but now I expect you are thinking of packing it in. I can see how awkward it must be for you. I'm offering you a way out so that you can leave immediately. I'll buy the business just as it stands, lock, stock and barrel. I'll give you a fair price. It's my way of making atonement.

"I know I haven't a particularly good reputation in Chellow. My adversaries call it sharp practice, maybe because they are jealous, I don't know, but I respected you, Leonie. I'm sorry it has to end like this. You didn't deserve it. If I thought there was the remotest possibility that you would accept I'd even offer to marry you."

"I haven't much to sell," she sighed ignoring his proposal of marriage. "The lease comes up for renewal shortly . . . "

"I know. I own the property, Leonie.

I didn't let on to you before in case you took umbrage. I'm prepared to buy the equipment — after all it is in excellent condition and well maintained. I think I know of someone who could make use of it."

* * *

A few days later Leonie went to Trenton to call at Andrews Electronics during business hours. She was dressed in her most conservative suit and had taken great pains to see that her hair was constrained firmly in place. It took a good deal of courage to summon up the will power to go but she was determined to act with decorum — even if others didn't.

"May I see Mr Andrews please?" she asked the young woman at the reception desk.

"I'm sorry but he's not here at the moment. Could anyone else be of assistance?"

Well she had tried she thought. She

hadn't wanted to confront him, but felt that it was the right and proper thing to do in the circumstances. Leonie handed the woman the envelope.

"Would you see he gets this when he returns. It's personal." With a grimace of a smile she turned to leave relieved that there had been no unpleasantness. She was thanking her lucky stars when a woman emerged from one of the offices at the rear of the building holding a sheaf of paperwork. Leonie's hands clenched tightly on to her brief case. The one person in the whole of Trenton whom she wished to avoid was heading in her direction.

"It's Miss Davis isn't it?" She gave Leonie a sugary smile. "Scott isn't here."

"So I have just been informed." Leonie stood erect and faced her — the woman who was causing her all the grief. This was the woman Scott was going to marry apparently. She would love to wipe that supercilious smile off her face.

"Can I help at all?"

"No thank you. I was . . . I came to say that 'Girl Friday' has closed down. Scott . . . Mr Andrews put a lot of work my way in the past, and I wanted to thank him personally before I left."

"I'm sure my fiancé was only too pleased to be able to help. He'll be sorry to have missed you. He's away in Australia at the moment, but I expect him back shortly. We can't have a wedding without the groom now can we?" She gave a tinkling little laugh which sent shivers down Leonie's spine.

"May I wish you both the best of luck?" Leonie murmured moving away. There was little point in starting an argument. Scott had obviously made his choice. She had her pride.

"Are you staying on in Chellow, Miss Davis?" Penny Scot walked with her towards the front entrance. Somehow Leonie sensed a wariness about the question. She paused with her hand on the door handle.

"No," she replied, determined to appear unruffled and serene. She wouldn't give this woman the satisfaction of seeing her demoralised.

"May I ask what you are planning to do next?"

"I'm taking a holiday before making any decision about my future. I have no ties."

That brought a relieved smile to Penny Scot's face. A victorious smile Leonie thought dismally. She would love to say something crushing and triumphant but could think of nothing.

7

EARLY in the morning before anyone else was about Leonie packed her clothes and the few possessions she was taking with her into the car and set off, Roy Clark generously having offered to store her surplus baggage until she had another place of her own. It was fortunate because it was amazing how much clutter she had collected over the years. Some things she was loath to part with, especially mementoes of Jolie and their time together.

She felt a bit of a coward because she hadn't announced to anyone else that she was leaving so precipitously, but she couldn't face the ignominy. She felt let down by the people of Chellow, especially the business people to whom she had given good service. After living in their midst for above twelve years it was going to feel dreadfully strange being anywhere else, but she couldn't remain if they believed such rumours about her and her family. It was no place for her if they were so narrow minded.

As Leonie motored north she thought how circumstances could change within a short period of time. She had never envisaged selling her business to Simon Dean of all people. Never in a month of Sundays. Simon had been the last person she would have wanted anything to do with, but he had arrived so fortuitously and offered her a way out of her predicament. She had wanted to throw it back in his face, but sense had prevailed. She couldn't pay the bills with what she was earning or could even remotely earn herself, so it wouldn't be long before she had to move out.

It galled her deeply to accept his offer but in the end she knew that it was the only sensible thing to do. At least it left her with sufficient money to make a complete break from Chellow and in view of Scott's impending nuptials that was upper-most in her mind.

If she could get far enough away she might be able to forget him and make a new life for herself. With all the outstanding debts paid she still had enough to keep herself for several months until she found alternative employment. She thanked her lucky stars for having been prudent enough to always have something in reserve.

* * *

Leonie arrived in the Lake District and booked into the first small hotel she saw with a vacancy sign outside. The weather was perfect but unfortunately she couldn't appreciate it or the splendid scenery, she was too wrapped up in her misery. For the time being it didn't matter where she was, nothing could dispel the heartache and despair — even such picturesque surroundings. The Lake District had always held great attraction for her, ever since she'd been taken there as a child on a day trip. She had been very young at the time but the memory still remained.

Gradually as the days passed she found some inner peace. She was used to her own company and found pleasure in walking the fells — it gave her time to evaluate her life. What should she do? Where should she go? In some ways the Lake District reminded her of Austria and that made her reflect on Giorgio, and whether he really meant his offer of a job. She didn't want to rush into making any major decisions. She felt she needed time to recover from such a disastrous six months. Oh, Jolie! Why did you have to go and leave me?

She began to put her life together with the help of two small children who were staying at the hotel — they befriended her. Paul and Tom's aunt and uncle owned the hotel, and since it was the height of the holiday season they were rushed off their feet, so the two children were at a loose end for a good deal of the time. Leonie offered to take them out for walks which was greatly appreciated by all concerned. The children helped take her mind of her troubles as together they explored the countryside.

Leonie took them on a motor launch on the lake and they visited the wildlife centre which was a huge success. They also paid a visit to the cottage where Beatrix Potter had lived because the children owned several of her story books and often asked Leonie to read them aloud.

"You know you may just be in the right place at the right time," the hotel owner said one evening as Leonie was about to retire to her room.

"How's that?" she asked with interest.

"How would you feel about looking after those two young imps for another couple of months?"

"Two months. Hmm, I don't know if I . . ."

"Let me explain," he went on. "Their mother's just had a major operation which is why they are staying with us for the time being. However, their father — my brother, is expected tomorrow to take them home, and then they are going to Spain for a couple of months so their mother can recuperate. Gerald, I know is looking for someone to go with them and help out generally. It wouldn't pay much but it shouldn't prove too onerous either.

"I just thought, since they seem to get on all right with you and you were talking about looking for a job . . . Anyway, think about it. Gerry will be here tomorrow and if you're interested I'll put in a good word for you. You've certainly taken a load of my shoulders these last few days."

"But you hardly know me," she protested.

"In this trade we get used to summing people up, and I reckon I'm a pretty good judge of character. They couldn't do better, I'm positive."

Leonie smiled inwardly wishing she had that same insight, it would have saved her a lot of anguish. She thanked him and said she'd think about it.

The next day Leonie was in the sun lounge reading when the two boys dragged their father in to see her. The man looked nothing like his brother. He seemed rather shy and slightly scruffy but Leonie also saw the tiredness in his eyes. Having heard about his wife's illness she realised what he must have been going through.

"Go on, daddy, ask her," Tom urged.

"Isn't she pretty, dad. She says she can type too," said Paul the elder of the two.

"You must be Miss Davis. I gather you are a cross between Mary Poppins and superwoman."

"Leonie, please," she said with an amused grin. "I've been pleased to have your children's company. They haven't been any trouble. If you must know they've taught me a thing or two."

Gerry Chandler took a seat and promptly sent the boys to the kitchen on an errand.

"My brother says that you have kept them out of mischief and instilled some manners into them. That is quite an achievement!"

"I think he's overestimating my abilities. I'd better come clean and say at the outset that I'm not a nanny or a nurse or even a cordon bleu cook."

"Well, I'll be equally honest and say that it's a relief to know that." He rubbed a hand along his thigh then beat a tattoo with his fingers. "The children simply need someone to keep an eye on them. My wife is getting better daily so shouldn't need any assistance other than perhaps a hand with the shopping and some general housework. We don't go in for exotic meals, just plain simple fair is preferred."

"What do you do, Mr Chandler?"

"Gerry, if you don't mind. Mr Chandler makes me sound like an old fuddy duddy. I'm a writer. Travel books. My brother tells me that you are looking for secretarial work. From the sound of things you are heaven sent. I guess it's a bit of a tall order at such short notice, but how do you feel about the job? I guess it's a bit of a cheek asking you, but I'm getting desperate. I don't want my wife taking up the reins too soon, and yet I can't cope on my own."

Leonie thought he looked a nice solid family man and felt comfortable with him. She decided instantly that it would be perfect from her own point of view. Two months would give her time to think about whether to contact Giorgio or not.

"I'm certainly prepared to give it a go if you are. I haven't anything lined up for the next couple of months, so the thought of spending them in Spain is very appealing."

"Could you possibly start at the end of the week?" he asked.

"Wouldn't you prefer to discuss it with your wife first? After all . . . "

"Cynthia will be delighted to find our problem so conveniently solved, especially as you already get on well with the boys. They can be a bit of a handful and my wife isn't up to coping with them full time just yet."

It was arranged for Leonie to travel down at the end of the week to their house in a village just north of Manchester. They were wanting to fly out to Spain the following week if possible so there was little time to lose.

* * *

Leonie arrived at the Chandler house the following Friday. It was an old house with quaintly shaped rooms and a large untidy garden. It had a warm friendliness about it, and when she met Cynthia she realised why.

"We've got the use of a villa in Spain," Cynthia Chandler explained over coffee. "It belongs to a friend of ours, and he lets us use it whenever we like. He bought it for when he retires, but so far finds he's too busy to use it much himself. Have you travelled much, Leonie?"

"Not a lot unfortunately. I've been to Spain a couple of times before as a tourist, and also to Austria, the latter on business though."

"You'll have you watch you don't burn. The sun can get quite fierce at this time of the year. Usually we go much later in the season, but Gerry insists we go now. Feels the sun will do me good. Fortunately the children take after their father and tan easily without burning, although I prefer to keep them covered all the same. I must get them some more T-shirts. I'm sure they seem to be growing by the minute."

Cynthia had taken to Leonie straight away. They had an immediate affinity for each other.

The time passed quickly as they prepared for the trip. Leonie and Cynthia making several forays into town to buy extra clothes for the boys and other requisites to take with them. It meant Leonie had little time to brood. Then it was time to head for the airport and Spain. Leonie felt a moment of almost panic when she entered the terminal building. The first thing she did was to scour the other travellers for Scott. The last time she had flown from there she had been accompanying him on what had been then a happy occasion. If only she had known what trouble was in store!

She wondered what he was doing now and whether he ever gave her a second thought. What had been his reaction when he received her letter? She had expected some sort of reply but had heard nothing. Fortunately with two young children to keep amused and entertained she hadn't time to let her thoughts wander too much. It still hurt though — the thought that she had so seriously misjudged him. He could have phoned. But to hear nothing —

The flight was without incident and they were soon driving away in the hire car to the villa in the sun. Being in another country helped Leonie come to terms better with her feelings, and she firmly pushed all thoughts of Chellow and Scott behind her. She felt she would never be able to trust a man in a romantic way again. Her feelings had misled her, but in future she would know better.

"That's the villa," pointed Tom jumping up and down with excitement. "I remember the red tiled roof and the balcony."

"I'm going to dive straight into the pool," said Paul. "I'm boiled alive."

"First you have to show Leonie where everything is," their father said drolly, "and what about all the unpacking?"

"We can do that later can't we? Leonie would love a swim wouldn't you?" The two children pleaded with her to say yes.

In the end Paul and Tom were allowed to swim while the grown ups wandered into the cool interior.

"I'll fetch the bags," said Gerry, "and then I'll show you round, Leonie. You go and rest, love," he urged his wife. "Leonie and I can manage. This heat will take some getting acclimatised to. I don't want you overdoing it."

The villa was spacious and modern with lovely views from most of the rooms. It was situated half way along a promontory which formed a tight little bay, and was only one of about half a dozen buildings on the outskirts of the village. Across the bay was another rocky headland reached by a stretch of white sandy beach. A few small boats were pulled up on to the shoreline but there were few people about. A wooden balcony ran the full length of the villa, and was bedecked with gaudy geraniums and trailing variegated ivy in large planters. Various sun loungers and chairs also littered the balcony which looked a pleasant place from which to enjoy the view.

"The children always have the room at the end of the landing, so I think you should have this one next to them," said Gerry depositing Leonie's cases on the bed. "There's a bathroom in between as you see. I hope you'll find everything satisfactory."

"It's marvellous," she said. "The children certainly seem to be at home already, just listen to them." Their happy squeals could be heard as they splashed happily in the pool below.

"They swim like fish thank goodness and the pool isn't very deep."

It was a super villa. The lounge was furnished sparingly and had a patio door opening on to a paved sitting-out area with the swimming pool immediately below. The kitchen, Leonie discovered, was large enough for the family to eat in and was equipped with all modern facilities.

"We should find a box of groceries," Cynthia said wanly standing by the patio door watching the children. "And fresh milk and orange juice. It was all arranged."

"Where is the nearest shop or supermarket?" Leonie asked checking out the store cupboard.

"Hardly a supermarket," Cynthia laughed, "but the shop in the village carries the basics, otherwise it's a ten mile round trip to the nearest town."

* * *

A week passed in no time — an extremely pleasant week of sun, sea and sand. Leonie enjoyed being part of the Chandler family. The children were no problem as all they wanted to do was spend their time in the water or on the beach. There was also a box full of games and children's books for the evenings or if the weather changed.

Leonie happily took to the warm sunshine and felt some of her old vigour returning. Cynthia unfortunately felt drained by the heat and rested in the shade with a book or some knitting most of the time. Gerry resolutely scribbled away in what would be the dining room. It was on the shady part of the house and Leonie felt sorry for him missing out on the sunshine.

She took her supervisory position seriously and never let the children out of her sight, which meant she had to spend a good deal of the time on the beach too. She had brought a couple of bikinis with her and also a one piece swim costume which she felt more appropriate for wearing in the children's presence. Most of the time she covered up with T-shirts and plenty of sun cream and made the children do likewise.

At times Leonie pondered on the possibility of becoming a children's nanny, and wondered what the training entailed and what the qualifications were. The thought of going back to being a secretary again wasn't so appealing as it once used to be.

"Would you like me to do some typing for you?" she asked Gerry one evening. "I feel a fraud being here enjoying myself, lolling about on the beach all day while you slave away." Cynthia had told her how worried she was about the amount of time he'd taken off when she was ill. After the hectic time Leonie had when she ran her own business this was a doddle, making her feeling guilty and she knew Gerry was pushed for time.

"Now that's an offer I won't refuse if you are sure you don't mind. I've a deadline to meet and I'm sadly behind hand already." Gerry accepted gratefully. "Just as well we brought the old portable. Think you can cope with its eccentricity? I had thought to find an agency in town. Are you sure you don't mind?"

"Typing is what I used to do for a living don't forget. I'd be delighted to do it. I'm more used to a computer these days, but I'll cope, don't worry."

So the days and weeks past in hazy, liberated friendliness. Leonie began to look tanned and healthy and gradually the strain lines disappeared from her face. She couldn't say she was exactly happy and she couldn't completely shut out all that had happened that year, but it was fading slightly. She found it difficult though to plan far ahead, the sun was soporific. Que sera sera she thought lazily. Chellow was a million miles away.

"You never talk about yourself, Leonie. Have you no family?" Cynthia asked her one morning as they prepared breakfast together.

"No. No family that I know of. For most of my life I lived in a children's home."

"Good heavens, you poor thing," said Cynthia. "How did you manage? I mean when you left . . . "

Leonie smiled — it was the usual reaction which was why she didn't often mention it. "It wasn't so dreadful. We used to live in Tideswell, but after my parents died I was sent to Chellow children's home. I'm not sure why. The people that ran it treated me well enough and I always had plenty of playmates — more than I wanted in fact.

"When it came time for me to leave the staff helped me find a job and a place to stay, so it wasn't so bad." She made light of her feelings, not wanting people to feel sorry for her. "I'm not a gregarious sort of person so I studied hard to become a secretary. I even took a bookkeeping course and eventually set up my own business in Chellow."

"Chellow? We know someone there. It's a lovely little town isn't it? So what happened to the business? Recession hit you? I know the publishing industry has been hit hard."

"Not exactly. I fell foul of some of the businessmen who got the wrong impression of what services I was selling!"

"Oh, my goodness," Cynthia gasped smothering a grin.

"Once the rumours spread the work disappeared so I couldn't carry on and everything fell apart," Leonie said sweeping back her hair which she had allowed to fall forward to hide her embarrassment. It was a condensed version of the truth at least.

"Being beautiful like you it must be difficult to make people take you seriously."

"I'm not beautiful," Leonie said in surprise.

"Go on. Take a good look at yourself in the mirror. I must admit I was wary of employing you when I first saw you, wondering if my marriage was safe. You manage to twist the boys round your little finger and I began to wonder about Gerry too."

"Now I know you're teasing me. You and Gerry have a wonderful marriage. He worships the ground you walk on. I've never seen him look at another woman."

"I know, but one can't afford to relax one's guard. Gerry's often remarked that he had a passion for redheads when he was young." Cynthia's grin showed there was no malice in her remarks. "No young man pining away then back in Chellow?"

"No. Men are the cause of all my trouble."

In some ways it was a relief to be able to talk about it to another woman. When Jolie was alive they had spent many hours discussing and pondering their personal problems — mainly Jolie's problems in those days. She missed her friend more each day — the companionship they had shared for so long. Leonie went on to relate how she'd met Scott. It was the first time she had spoken about what had happened and suddenly it all came pouring out. How she'd lost her close friend and when she'd tried to avenge her death it had so badly misfired.

"You've had a poor year so far haven't you?" Cynthia commiserated. "It must have been dreadful for you all alone like that."

"Yes it was, but it's getting better now though. Ever since I met Paul and Tom and through them you and Gerry. You've salvaged some of my faith in human nature. You know, Gerry never asked for a reference or anything."

"You've certainly made a big hit with our family. I don't know how we'd have coped without you these last few weeks. It's a pity writing isn't more rewarding and we could employ you for longer."

"Thanks. The boys will soon be back at school and you are almost back up to strength according to Gerry, so I realise that my services are no longer needed. I've really enjoyed looking after the boys, it hasn't felt like work at all."

Cynthia cleared her throat hesitantly as she popped toast into the toaster.

"Forgive me for being personal, Leonie, but you are pregnant aren't you?"

Leonie almost dropped the jug of orange juice she was taking from the fridge.

"How did you know?"

"I've been through it twice myself don't forget," Cynthia replied. "Call it an educated guess. I wasn't absolutely sure."

"Good heavens. I suppose I should have told you. I didn't mean any deception. But I didn't . . . "

"It makes no difference to me."

"Does Gerry know?"

"No, I don't think so, but he would think the same as me, I'm sure. You will make a wonderful mother, you're so good with the children. It's just that I wondered what you are planning to do when we get home, since you say you have no family."

"I don't intend keeping the baby," Leonie said quietly.

Cynthia looked startled. "Why ever not? Plenty of women manage to . . . "

"I'm thinking about what is best for the child. I was brought up in a children's home don't forget. I want my child to have a proper loving family — a mother and a father which is something I can't give him. I wish it were not so, but there it is."

"You'll change you're mind," Cynthia said briskly. "When the time comes you'll not be able to go through with it. It's not that easy."

"Yes, I will. I have to for the child's sake. I have to be strong and put aside my personal feelings."

* * *

The holiday was drawing to a close. One more week and they would be leaving. It had been wonderful while it lasted and Leonie felt stronger both emotionally and physically. For a change Gerry took a day off from his writing and they spent the whole day on the beach together. It was fun and it would have been one of the best days ever — except for Leonie's unexpected visitor.

Near lunch time Cynthia took the boys for a walk along the beach seeking interesting shells to decorate the sand castle they had built. Leonie remained behind with Gerry relaxing in the warm sunshine cogitating on what she was going to do when she returned to England. Now that it was imminent she had to start planning her future, or at least what she was going to do for the next six months.

Wearing one of her bikinis for a change she stretched out on a towel to top up her sun tan conscious that if they were to remain much longer she would have had to buy one a size larger. Dimly she heard the sea lapping the shore and birds wheeling overhead and wished that she didn't have to go back to England because then her problems would become a reality. Being in Spain one felt cut off from problems and could pretend they didn't exist for most of the time. Back in England she would be on her own again and that seemed a bleak prospect.

"I feel as if I could do with some oil on, my shoulders are beginning to burn. Would you mind, Leonie." Gerry broke into her train of thoughts.

"Sure," she said. "Gosh, but it is warm isn't it? I'm going to miss this. On the radio I heard that it is pouring down in London and has been for two days now."

She unearthed the suntan lotion from amongst the beach paraphernalia and proceeded to spread it over Gerry's back as he lay prone on the beach. She was completely absorbed in the task, making sure that she did a good job as usual. She was used to ladling it on the children and treated Gerry in much the same way. She was unaware of the man approaching. It was only when he spoke that she became conscious of him. Immediately the blood rushed to her head. She felt quite faint.

"Good morning, Miss Davis. Providing your special kind of service as usual I see."

That voice! The voice she had longed to hear for so long now that she had given up hope. A voice she'd yearned to comfort her, but had never expected to hear again, and especially not on a beach in Spain. Squinting in the bright sunlight she stared up at him trying to recover her senses.

"Scott," she gulped drying her hands on a towel. "What are you doing here? How did you . . . " She was so pleased to see him after all this time that she could even overlook the teasing remark.

She saw from the look on his face though that he wasn't kidding — he was furious, she had never seen him look so angry.

"I see Penny was right. I've wasted my time coming after you," he continued icily. "You had me completely fooled."

"Now, see here . . . "

"It's all right, Gerry. Scott makes a habit of jumping to wrong conclusions about me. He never learns." Leonie sadly hung her head in dismay. He hadn't come to tell her the good news she was hoping for. For an instant she thought perhaps . . .

"My first impression was obviously the correct one. You're nothing but a . . . "

"That's enough. I'll not have you speaking about Leonie like that," Gerry interrupted, angrily leaping to her defence. "Who do you think you are? You obviously don't know her like I do. I've never met a more trustworthy, competent, truthful young woman. Do you think I'd have her taking care of my children otherwise?"

"Children!" Scott gazed around smirking. "I don't see any."

"They're over . . . "

Leonie scrambled to her feet, red faced she glared angrily at Scott. "I don't know why you bothered coming. I presume you got my letter and since . . . "

"Letter? What letter?" he interrupted.

"The one I left at your flat."

"I haven't seen any letter." He sighed — a deep weary sigh and ran a hand through his hair. He wore it longer now and in a way it suited him she thought. He looked thinner though — she would even go so far as to say gaunt, and he was pale by comparison to other occupants of the beach. Harassed described him best, as if he'd spent too much time behind his desk worrying about the business. Maybe Penny was badgering him about the wedding plans too.

"How did you find me?" Leonie asked clutching her arms around her waist in an attempt to hide her slightly rounded stomach.

"Tina," he snapped, shrugging his shoulders dismissively. "When I couldn't find you in Chellow I went looking for her. I had no idea you'd packed up and left town. Why on earth didn't you tell me you had problems? I told you I'd help. Tina didn't know where you'd gone but promised to let me know if she heard from you." He scowled down at the sand seemingly having difficulty in believing what he saw. "Why did you run away, Leonie? I told you I needed time — time to sort things out. Couldn't you have waited? I thought . . . "

"I didn't leave voluntarily," Leonie almost sobbed, but managed with some difficulty to keep her composure. He still looked desirable in casual jeans and open neck shirt, just like he had in Austria, but she knew she couldn't trust him and she couldn't trust her own instincts either. This time she wouldn't allow her heart to rule her head. She couldn't afford to let him know how she still felt about him.

"I was forced to leave as no doubt Tina would have told you. I don't know how you have the gall to come here after . . . after . . . " Her eyes blazed with anger. Her fury quite apparent. It was the best way and the only way for her to deal with the situation.

"What the hell did I do?" He seemed totally unprepared for such animosity.

"Don't tell me you didn't see me at the Chase Hotel that day. You were dining there with Miss Scot — your fiancée."

"It wasn't how it looked. Penny arranged it as a surprise — a birthday luncheon. It was no big deal. Of course I saw you — you were with that damned fellow Dean. That was why I didn't come over."

"And you thought I had arranged to spend the afternoon with him I presume?"

"That was the way it looked," he retorted. "It's what Penny thought too.

She remarked on it. It was Penny that drew my attention to you as a matter of fact. She saw you kissing him in the foyer."

"I did nothing of the sort. As it happens I went there thinking I was visiting a bone fide client. I had no idea it was Simon Dean I was to meet. He gave a false name. He got short shrift from me when I learned how I'd been tricked I can tell you."

"So why did you sell your business to him?" Scott countered.

Leonie sniffed contemptuously. "I hadn't much choice in the matter. I had no other option but to sell at the best possible price and get out in the circumstances. It so happened that Simon offered me extremely generous terms. He was always there when I needed him, not like some I could mention."

"I say again, what did I do?" Scott growled.

Leonie took a step back and with hands on hips glared at him. She was so incensed that she nearly exploded with anger. "You want me to spell it out?" she yelled. "Well, it so happens that Roy Clark is a very good friend of mine. He runs Clarks the engineering firm in Chellow as you must already know since he's done work for you in the past. He plucked up the courage to tell me what had been going on behind my back. He told me who was behind the malicious scheme to run me out of town.

"Silly me, I thought it was all Simon Dean's doing, which is what you wanted me to believe all along, wasn't it? Then I heard how you put pressure on Roy — told him not to use my services. He hadn't wanted to tell me but he couldn't afford not to. When I asked him why, he told me that otherwise the work he got from your firm would dry up and he would be put out of business. Talk about bribery and corruption — "

"He said what!"

That seemed to shake him.

"You heard, and don't look so amazed. He wasn't my only client to be put under the same sort of constraint by you and your precious girl friend, and all the time I thought it was Simon that had taken the hump. He at least came and apologised to me for telling Penny about . . . about my father," she said bleakly. "It wasn't him that spread the gossip."

"Gossip! What gossip? I haven't a clue what you're talking about, Leonie. I never threatened Clark. Why the devil should I do such a thing?"

"I saw the proof," Leonie said snidely. "I know your signature when I see it. When I learned the truth I called to see you to demand an explanation, only you weren't available. You were out of the country according to your fiancée. Miss Scot very politely suggested that it was time I made myself scarce as far as you were concerned. Her claws were definitely showing, as if she wanted to scratch my eyes out. She gleefully informed me of your forthcoming nuptials."

Scott swore under his breath and looked as if he'd like to commit murder. "When did all this happen?" he asked through gritted teeth.

"What does it matter. Just leave me alone, Scott. Go back to Penny and your cosy existence. Jolie was right, I'm not cut out to be a business woman. I'm not devious and manipulative. I believe in playing fair. You didn't even come and ask me if what they were saying was true. Just go, I never want to see you again." Dropping her sunglasses on the towel she ran into the sea where she could cry to her heart's content.

8

LATER, back at the villa Leonie rinsed out the bathing costumes and hung them out to dry. Several hours had elapsed which had given her time to calm down, but she was still trying desperately to come to terms with her disillusionment. She knew Gerry would have told Cynthia about the fracas, but so far it hadn't been mentioned. Cynthia joined her in the kitchen ready to prepare the evening meal and straightaway commiserated with her now they were alone.

"Gerry told me about the scene down on the beach. Are you all right, Leonie? It must have been awful for you."

"Sure. I'm fine, never better. At least I now know where I stand."

"Who was he? The baby's father?"

"Hmm."

"I take it he doesn't know?"

"No, apparently he doesn't. Please, you won't tell him will you? He must never find out."

"I think you're making a big mistake, but it's your own affair. I couldn't interfere anyway since all I know is he's called Scott and lives somewhere near Chellow. According to Gerry he looked liked a prize fighter snapping and snarling at you. Want to tell me what went wrong?"

Leonie sighed and took a deep breath to stop herself from breaking down in tears. She picked up a kitchen knife and began slicing the cucumber to go with the salad.

"For the first time in my life I did something that I'd seen others do and vowed I'd never fall into the same trap. I fell hook, line and sinker for Scott from the very first moment we met. I felt it was kismet. He said he felt the same way and I like a fool believed him. I knew he was kind of engaged, but he said it was only a temporary business commitment, would you believe and not to be taken seriously!"

Cynthia put a hand on her arm as if she understood. "So you fell in love. It happens all the time. That is something you can't legislate for you know. Take me and Gerry for instance. My mother said it would never last. She couldn't see how I could possibly fall for someone who would be under my feet all day and without a steady income such as a writer. It takes all sorts — "

Leonie continued chopping the cucumber concentrating hard on what she was doing as if her life depended upon it. "I never thought that he could be so hypocritical though," she murmured. "He once had the nerve to say that he thought women were devious."

"What did he want?" Cynthia asked cautiously. "Why did he come after you?"

Leonie nibbled her lip for a moment. She had thought of nothing else since the confrontation with Scott. Why had he come? Was it true that he hadn't received her letter? He must surely have got the earrings.

"To tell you the truth I don't know why he did come. We argued right from the word go."

"Maybe he does know — about the baby I mean."

"He said he hadn't received my letter so I don't see how he could, unless — Well, it doesn't matter now anyway."

"So you did write and tell him?"

"Oh yes." Leonie sighed. "I felt I ought to be completely honest about it. He told me once about his sister who had been married for four years with no sign of pregnancy. That seemed to bother him. He said his mother looked forward to having grandchildren to stay, but from they way he spoke . . .

"I wondered vaguely if perhaps Scott thought he might not be able to have children, as if maybe they both . . . I wrote to set his mind at rest on that score — at least that was my explanation at the time. I didn't want to put any pressure on him — to get married or anything. I went round to his flat because, I suppose, I simply wanted to tell someone," Leonie added lamely.

"That's quite understandable. I know how I felt when I first knew I was pregnant. I didn't know how to contain my excitement. I wanted the whole wide world to know and couldn't wait to wear maternity clothes. But if you say you wrote to him, how come he never received the letter?"

"That is the mystery. I was going to post it, but changed my mind. Instead I decided to drive to his flat. I hoped to see him, to tell him properly and explain how I felt. It was difficult to put into words. If he wasn't in I was going to put the letter under his door hoping that he would contact me as soon as he got it. He was travelling about quite a bit so I didn't know when he would be home.

"Anyway, when I arrived I heard someone in the flat. I was feeling terribly nervous. I didn't know how he would take my news. So you can imagine my horror when Penny — his girl friend — came to the door. She looked quite at home there," Leonie added dryly. "Before I knew what was happening she had taken the letter from me and said she would give it to Scott. She implied he was in the shower."

Leonie pulled a face and paused for a moment. "I rather hoped that Scott would at least have the decency to come and see me once he'd read it. It wasn't as if I was expecting him to do anything. I just thought he ought to know."

"So why didn't you tell him all that today?"

"He assumed the worst about me as usual. Caught me in the act of massaging your husband with sun tan oil!"

"Good grief. I wish I'd been there.

I'd have given him a piece of my mind."

"If you'd been there maybe we could possibly have had a normal conversation for a change."

"Hmm. I see what you mean. I still think you ought to have tried . . . "

"It wouldn't have made any difference. I shall have to go through with my original plan. He's obviously still seeing Penny and I made it plain that I didn't feel it appropriate for us to continue seeing each other until he'd resolved that particular problem. Maybe he never had any intention of finishing with her — I just don't know.

"Anyway when he gets back home, no doubt Penny will fill him in about my past and then he'll be relieved that he made me no commitment."

"I don't see . . . Just because . . . "

Leonie shook her head. "No, I didn't mean because I was brought up in a children's home. Until I was nine I had a happy, normal childhood." Leonie gazed out of the window seeking to clarify her thoughts. "My mother who was never a well person spent much of the time in and out of various hospitals unfortunately. My father was a solicitor and spent a fortune trying to find a cure for her complaint without success. It turned out though that it wasn't only *his* own money he used. He *borrowed* clients investments too.

"It was all reported in the newspaper in typical graphic, gory details — you know the sort of thing. When my mother died they said he killed himself by driving off a cliff, but I know that wasn't true. They said it was because he couldn't face up to what he'd done and made him out to be a heartless, cruel father as well as a criminal."

"Oh, my dear, how terrible. What a dreadful thing to happen."

"He wasn't like that. I know he wasn't. He was a good man — a wonderful, loving father to me. I was named after him. His name was Leon but everyone called him Leo. On the night he died — it was shortly after my mother's death, we had gone to our favourite place up on the cliff top at Tideswell. We sat for a while watching the sea, and I could tell that he had something to tell me. He looked worried. He told me eventually that he had sold our house. He explained everything — told me that we needed the money to pay the hospital bills so we couldn't afford to stay in our present home. Since there were only the two of us he said it was better to move into a flat which would be easier to look after.

"I remember telling him that I would take care of him and that he wasn't to worry, that we didn't need such a big place. I could do the housework after school and we could do the shopping together at the weekend.

"He looked much happier after that and suggested we went for a walk. We . . . we got out of the car to go down to the shore — something we often did. As I got out my scarf blew from my hands and I ran to retrieve it. I heard my father call out. The next thing I saw was my father racing to catch up and get back in at the driver's door. The car was rolling away down the hill, gathering speed alarmingly. The handbrake was faulty — it had played up the previous week but dad hadn't had time to have it fixed — what with everything. He died trying to stop the car going over the cliff."

"And none of this came out at the time?"

"No. The first I knew of what had been reported was when I left school years later. I was going to get a job in Tideswell, but the matron at the home suggested, very gently, that perhaps it wasn't a good idea to go back there. I remember saying that it was my home town and that I should face up to my nightmares, but she still insisted that it would be wiser for me not to return. She was quite firm about it, but wouldn't elaborate further which aroused my suspicions. I decided to visit the town — the first time since the accident, and I checked back in the local paper to see how it had been reported. I was horrified by what I read.

"It was too late obviously to rectify the damage done to my father's good name. Nothing would bring him back, but nobody had thought to ask me what had happened at the time. I was only nine years old and traumatised I suppose, so they sent me to Chellow out of harm's way."

"And you believe this Penny Scot blackened your character because of something that was wrongly reported over twelve years ago? Surely Scott wouldn't believe — he wouldn't take any notice of a newspaper article. Besides, it was none of your doing. No-one could blame you, Leonie."

"The people of Chellow are extremely narrow minded. The report made out that my father was a thief and totally dishonest, so of course I am not to be trusted likewise. That is how they will see it. Like father like daughter and all that, and as far as they are concerned it was all down in black and white. I'm not sure why Penny disliked me so much except because of my association with Scott.

"I would have stuck it out in Chellow and shown them that I could take it, but as it happened I was made a tempting offer for the business from Scott's hated rival which somehow salved my pride. Then, of course thcrc's the baby. I would be tarred as a scarlet woman wouldn't I? As an unmarried mother I would definitely be an undesirable in their midst. They would have a field day at my expense."

"Scott ought to know that he is to become a father you know. Maybe . . . "

"No. I've made one bad mistake already, I won't compound it by spoiling my child's future. This baby deserves much better parents and I'm determined to see that he gets them. Scott would only think I was being a typically devious female. He's had plenty of experience of those apparently. Besides, it didn't look as if he'd heard the latest gossip about my past and when he does he'll probably think it's good riddance. No, I've made up my mind."

Cynthia pursed her lips. "I must say I'm surprised that you didn't take precautions. You are such a level headed person, Leonie. I wouldn't have thought of you making a mistake like that."

"Oh, but it was genuine mistake. Honestly. I had never been interested in that sort of relationship before. I went out with men a few times of course, usually escorts that Jolie arranged, but never anything serious. It was only when I met Scott — he was different. For some reason I decided to take Jolie's contraceptive pills. I had a sort of feeling that . . . well . . . you know."

"And you hadn't been taking them long enough to take effect?"

Leonie nodded. "It was my own silly

fault you see. I can't blame Scott. He did ask."

"I think you are letting your poor childhood recollections colour your judgement a little too much. I can understand it of course, even though I can't imagine what it must be like not to have family to turn to. If there is any way I can help at any time you will ask won't you? I hope you will keep in touch when we get back to England. I'd like to hear how you get on."

"Thank you for your understanding. I am grateful for your support and advice, even though it doesn't look as if I'm prepared to heed it. Some people might think I am taking the coward's way out."

"I still believe you'll find when the time comes that you'll not be able to give up your baby as easily as you imagine. So shall we wait and see? You've no need to make such major decisions yet a while. When is the baby due?"

* * *

Four days later they were back in England. A dull, wet England and a somewhat depressing one. Leonie's spirits plummeted. She had no home, no family and suddenly the future loomed frighteningly before her. In Spain she had felt quite calm about her situation, but now she realised how dreadfully alone she was.

Cynthia coerced her into staying with them until she found somewhere else to stay but she didn't want to intrude on their goodwill for long. Besides, they would need the spare bedroom for when Gerry's parents came to stay. Fortunately Leonie found somewhere fairly quickly — a holiday cottage to let in a village some little distant from Chellow which she felt would do nicely. She only needed it until after the baby was born and then she intended emigrating. She had in mind to see if Giorgio meant his offer of a job after all, and in which case she would brush up on her German during the next few months.

The cottage was basic but adequate and the beauty as far as Leonie was concerned was that no-one in the village knew anything about her. It was only four miles to the nearest town so once she had her computer set up she could perhaps do some part time secretarial work which would eke out her finances. With that in mind she wrote to Roy Clark to let him know that she would be calling to collect the things he was storing for her.

Roy wrote back telling her not to bother making the trip, that he would bring them in the van the next weekend. Leonie was relieved because she hadn't been looking forward to returning to Chellow but hadn't felt like imposing on his generosity. It was now October and she was looking definitely pregnant — at least it was obvious to her.

* * *

Leonie settled in and made friends with the next door neighbour who happened to be the owner of the cottage. Mrs Cherry was an elderly widow, inquisitive and an incessant chatterbox, but helpful too in a motherly sort of way. She took Leonie under her wing and persuaded her to see their local GP when next he came to the village on his rounds.

Mrs Cherry's family lived a long way away so she rarely saw them and was thrilled to have Leonie to fuss over. Leonie wasn't sure how to react such overwhelming friendliness, it was so very different from what she'd experienced in Chellow. She had a hard job explaining why she wasn't buying too many baby accessories. She didn't feel she could tell her neighbour that she had no intention of keeping the baby. She would never have heard the end of it, instead she began knitting a shawl from a pattern Mrs Cherry loaned her.

* * *

The next Saturday morning a van rolled up outside as Leonie was about to go for her morning constitutional to collect the milk from the village shop. She could have it delivered but preferred to go and collect it. It meant she had a purpose for leaving her hideaway. She knew she couldn't stay inside out of sight for the next three months, much as she felt she would like to, and the exercise did her good.

"Tina! What brings you here?" she shrieked in alarm. She had been expecting Roy who would have been the soul of discretion, but once Tina knew of her condition she guessed the news would soon spread throughout the whole of Chellow and that was the last thing she wanted.

"Your goods and chattels, ma'am." Tina grinned mischievously. "I said I'd do Roy a favour. Don has gone to a football match so I thought I'd come to see you. What's this?" she asked gazing at Leonie's bulging tummy.

"The word is pregnant," Leonie said with a sigh, realising that it was too late to put on a looser smock, the damage was already done. "Let's get this lot unloaded before my next door neighbour comes to investigate. She's quite nosy. I'll give you a hand."

"Not in your condition you won't. You go and put the kettle on while I carry everything in. I won't have you lifting anything heavy." Tina masterfully shepherded Leonie back inside.

By the time the coffee was made Tina had unpacked the van and was wandering round the cottage. She flopped down on the sofa. "So, what gives?" she quizzed. "Who's the father?"

Instead of answering Leonie asked a question of her own. "I have a bone to pick with you, Tina. Why did you give Scott Andrews my address in Spain? I told you I wanted no-one to know my whereabouts."

"Oh, he found you did he. He nearly went frantic when he found you'd left Chellow without a forwarding address. It was lucky you sent me that postcard. I didn't think you meant to include him as well. Besides, he's from Trenton not Chellow."

"Of course I meant him," she snapped. "It was because of him that I was forced to sell the business, you idiot."

"Rubbish."

"It's not rubbish. If you must know, he told me that he would do anything to keep his company, and apparently the only way he could achieve that was by marrying Penny Scot. He was the one making trouble all the time, not Simon Dean, I suppose at Miss Scot's instigation."

Tina shook her head in disbelief. "I don't believe a word of it. He's not like that. Besides he hasn't married Penny Scot. The last I heard was that there was ructions at the firm and Miss Scot flew off in a huff. According to Roy,

Scott and Penny had an unholy row and Scott threatened legal proceedings if she so much as set foot in the office again, so I guess the wedding's off."

This was all news to Leonie.

"How come you get to chat to Roy so much?"

"Oh, didn't I tell you. After you left in such a hurry I decided to do some part time work — just to keep my hand in sort of. I visited some of your old reliable customers and Roy took me on. I only go a few hours a week and I'm really enjoying it — all those hunky men in the works you know." She laughed at Leonie's grunt of disapproval. "When Roy got your note I volunteered to come, and here I am."

"Thanks for that anyway. I wasn't looking forward to making the trip."

"So tell me about the baby. When is it due?"

"January," Leonie said with a weary sigh. "Another three months."

Tina counted off on her fingers. "If I

can count correctly that makes it about the time of your trips to Austria."

"OK. I suppose since you've already guessed, but I want you to promise that you won't tell a living soul."

"My lips are sealed, Boss. Promise."

"I don't want to have to move again until after the baby is born, and then as soon as possible I'm leaving for Austria." Make what you like of that Leonie thought.

"Say no more, a nod's as good as a wink. I guess you want the baby to be born British. I know I would. I only wish it were me in your condition."

Tina stayed for lunch and helped Leonie set up the computer. She was a great help and Leonie appreciated her blithe good humour. In a way it was good to hear all that had been going on in Chellow, all the gossip and rumours that were going the rounds. Much as she hated to admit it she missed Chellow. It had been her home for so long that she missed its familiarity.

During lunch Tina told her about the scheme that Simon Dean had to pull down her old office building and put up a self service grocery store.

"Apparently he'd acquired a great deal of property round about but needed 'Girl Friday' because of its frontage onto the main street. It will be a gold mine if he gets planning permission," Tina remarked knowingly. "I always thought he was behind our trouble. He came along with his marvellous offer at just the right moment if you remember. I never trusted him. His eyes are too close together for a start."

"What a strange expression. Perhaps you're right though, Tina, I wouldn't know. He used to make me feel uncomfortable — the way he looked at me. And maybe I have misjudged Scott Andrews, but it's all water under the bridge now. I've had enough of Chellow to last a lifetime."

* * *

During the next week Leonie thought a lot about what Tina had told her. In some ways it gave her food for hope but then sense prevailed. Scott had at no time suggested marriage with her. He was obviously in the same mould as Simon — not a family man, he liked to play the field. He would probably feel trapped by such a commitment as marriage and a family.

She didn't like the idea of forcing him into something he might regret even though she loved him, that was no basis for a happy marriage and her baby deserved *two* loving parents. Besides, he always thought the worst of her, always jumping to conclusions far too readily. He probably wouldn't accept that he was the father. Better to try to forget him if that was possible.

Cynthia wrote asking how she was coping and invited her to spend Christmas with them. That cheered Leonie up enormously. It gave her something to plan ahead for. She hadn't been looking forward to Christmas — the first one without Jolie, and had anticipated spending it alone.

The next time Cynthia wrote was to say that they knew of a young couple who were wanting to adopt a baby and was she interested in meeting them. They were friends of their neighbours actually. They desperately wanted a baby and it appeared they couldn't have them themselves; they had been trying for a long time without success.

Leonie wrote back to say that she was grateful for the their kind interest in her situation and would bear them in mind, but she didn't really want to know anything about the people who finally adopted her baby. That way she couldn't keep checking up on them, it was to be a clean break.

She didn't want to think about such things yet. The more the time went by the more difficult she realised it was going to be to part with her baby as Cynthia had shrewdly predicted. It would have been all right if Scott knew and wanted to help support it but she couldn't manage on her own. Not to give it the best possible life. She spent long hours wondering whether she was doing the right thing. Several times she started to write to Scott but the letters were never posted. The computer was idle and she made no move to find work of any kind. The shawl was progressing at a snail's pace.

The time until Christmas would have dragged if it hadn't been for Tina and Mrs Cherry. Leonie's neighbour called in almost daily and Leonie realised that she was probably lonely and tried not to feel irritated by her apparent nosiness. She obviously meant well and at least she broke up the otherwise dull monotony. Occasionally Leonie wished that she had the telephone installed so that she could talk to friends whenever she was feeling particularly lonely but it hardly seemed worth it for such a short lease.

Tina came quite often and she welcomed her visits because she brought news of the goings on in Chellow.

She also kept Leonie informed about Scott. Whether deliberate or not she wasn't sure.

"How come you know so much about what is going on at Andrews Electronics?" Leonie asked her one day.

"Well, Roy does a lot of work for them now, and Jane — you remember her, she works full time there, so we often have a chat. Scott is working like a Trojan apparently, working all hours God sends."

"So Clarks is prospering is it?" Leonie quickly changed the subject.

"I'll say. Roy was only remarking the other day that now Scott has full control of his firm things have really taken off. Clarks get a lot of orders from Andrews Electronics and Roy is thinking about expanding on the strength of it."

"Scott finally bought Penny Scot off then?"

"So it would appear."

9

LEONIE was woken one morning a few days before Christmas by someone thumping noisily on her front door. It was still quite early and it took her a little while to grasp what was going on. Recently she'd experienced difficulty in getting to sleep which usually meant she woke late and got up leisurely — she had nothing pressing normally to get up for.

"Leonie, Leonie, wake up." It was Tina causing a great hullabaloo.

Leonie pulled on her dressing gown and hurried barefoot down to let her in, wondering what catastrophe had happened to bring her all the way there at that time of morning.

"I wish you'd got the phone installed," Tina reproached her. "How are you going to get help if anything happens to you in the middle of the night?"

"Mrs Cherry is on the phone. She's promised to ring for an ambulance if one is required," Leonie said calmly. "Now what's the fuss about. I'm sure you didn't drive all the way here to reprimand me for not having a telephone."

"It's Scott Andrews. I thought you'd want to know what's happened straight away. Heaven knows how long it would take for the news to percolate to this out of the way place."

"Scott! Why? What's happened to him?" Leonie sat down abruptly, her mouth dry with apprehension. It had to be something extremely serious to bring Tina out at that time of morning. Surely he couldn't be . . .

"He's in hospital, that's what. He tackled a couple of thugs breaking into his works and they set about him good and proper."

"How . . . how badly is he hurt?" The words came out hardly above a whisper.

"One had a baseball bat I gather and

wielded it with some force. Apparently Scott is lucky to be alive." Tina went on. "He must have been lying unconscious for quite a time before someone discovered him, even though the burglar alarm was ringing. Nobody took any notice as usual. Eventually a well meaning citizen called the police about the racket and they sent someone to investigate. They found him in a pool of blood and the place ransacked."

"He's going to be all right though isn't he?" Leonie was dithering with shock, fearful that Scott may die and never know that he was to become a father. She should have told him when she had the chance.

"Jane said he's in a coma and that is why I came haring out here. He's asking for you, Leonie."

"Rubbish. Why should he ask for me?" Leonie realised that she was giving herself away and her true feelings for Scott were showing. Now she tried to put on a less concerned attitude. She felt she had convinced Tina that her baby's father was Austrian.

"Maybe it's a quirky reaction or something, the Andrews family don't know, but they asked Jane if she knew of anyone called Leonie. She immediately got in touch with me. There aren't many people around called Leonie. Well, since you swore me to silence I haven't breathed a word about your whereabouts, but in the circumstances, I thought . . . "

"What do you expect me to do? I can't go dashing to his bedside — especially in my condition."

"But he needs you. Do you think I'd have come if I didn't think it was vital. You wouldn't want to have his death on your conscience would you, and he might die. He's been under a lot of pressure lately, and has lost a lot of weight. His mother is extremely worried. I didn't think you were so heartless."

She turned and hurried over to the door obviously furious with Leonie's reaction.

"I don't know why he should ask for me," Leonie muttered.

"Neither do I," she snapped, "but he's been unconscious for hours and the only word he's uttered was your name. I would have thought . . . oh never mind. I guess I shouldn't have come."

Tina stormed out of the cottage, but before she drove away Leonie hurried after her quite oblivious of her bare feet on the cold doorstep.

"Where is he? What hospital?"

* * *

Two hours later Leonie drove into the Trenton District Hospital car park. She was a bundle of nerves as she walked towards the front entrance. She hated hospitals, they had too many unhappy memories for her.

At the reception desk they told her where to find Scott and she walked with as much dignity as she could muster down the corridors, hastily pulling her voluminous coat around her. She located the private wing and a nurse pointed her in the direction of Scott's room.

Slowly she pushed the door open, prepared for a speedy exit if necessary, she wasn't sure why. All was silent and strangely peaceful. A diminutive, but immaculately dressed, grey haired lady rose from her vigil at the bedside.

Leonie quietly closed the door and turned, quickly scanning the room for other visitors — there were none. She walked nervously towards the woman, but couldn't stop herself from glancing at the bed where Scott lay motionless. She hardly recognised him. Her heart was in her mouth at the sight of him. She braced herself to greet the woman. She looked so petite and delicate that for a moment Leonie couldn't credit that she was Scott's mother until she saw her eyes. Despite her obvious anxiety they were exactly like Scott's — she was her baby's grandmother. A knot formed in her stomach. She felt guilty and not able to face her so she approached the bedside.

"Come and take a seat, my dear." Mrs Andrews indicated the chair she had vacated. "You must be Leonie. I didn't realise — nobody told me you were pregnant. It was good of you to come in the circumstances."

"How is he?" Leonie asked almost in a whisper. Scott lay so still and pale; nothing like the strong, vital, virile man she knew. He was so battered, bruised and bandaged that she felt it incredible that he had survived the horrific attack.

"They say he's comfortable!" the woman remarked sourly. "I've never heard such rubbish. I'm jolly sure Scott wouldn't agree if he could speak." She dabbed her eyes with a damp handkerchief. "If only he would. Please would you mind staying with him for a moment? I must go and ring my daughter. I don't like leaving him for a second in case he wakes up. I won't be long. He's not said anything for ages."

When Mrs Andrews left the room Leonie gazed down at Scott willing him to open his eyes. She wanted to see those sparkling blue eyes again, see them glinting with mischief and affection like she'd first seen them. If only they could turn the clock back she would react so differently. Why hadn't she believed him when he said Penny meant nothing to him? Why hadn't she trusted him? She should have followed her own first instincts? Surely it wasn't too late to put things right between them? It couldn't be!

Drawing the chair up closer she took her place at the bedside and stretched out to stroke his hand. As soon as she touched his fingers she felt a faint movement. It was so slight that she wondered if she had been mistaken, but it gave her hope.

"Scott, it's Leonie," she whispered hoping she wasn't clutching at straws. "Can you hear me? I gather you were asking for me. Well, I'm here now and I've got something to tell you.

Something I tried to tell you before but it rather looks as if you never received my letter. I don't expect you to do anything about it, but I thought you ought to know that you are going to be a father."

His fingers curled round and ever so slightly squeezed her own. It gave her renewed hope.

"I haven't told your mother anything about us, so if you like, we can keep it a secret — our secret." Probably Penny knows though she thought. She must have read the letter and deliberately kept the news from him. That must be what happened.

"I was going to have the baby adopted, but maybe we could talk about that when you are better. You must get well again, Scott for all our sakes. You can't leave me now — I want the chance — I want you to know that you shouldn't believe all you read in the newspapers or the scandal that spread so contagiously about my family. I'd like to explain to you before you decide anything else. I promise I'm not trying to manipulate you, I just want you to know the truth. I hope you'll believe me despite what you may have heard to the contrary.

"My father never swindled anyone. He may have borrowed some money which strictly speaking wasn't his, but he had already sold our house to repay it. Also, he never committed suicide. The papers had it all wrong. He loved my mother passionately, but he also loved me and had no intention of leaving me on my own. He would never do anything to hurt me like that.

"I think you would have liked him. I know he would have liked you. I love you, Scott. Please believe that. I always have, ever since we met at the Flamingo Club all those months ago. I suppose you were hurt because I returned the earrings. I'm sorry I did that now. I thought — well it doesn't matter what I thought. Remember how it was with us in Austria? I wish we could go back and start all over again, only I realise that isn't possible. Forgive me, Scott."

"Having a cosy little chat are we?" The cold, cynical voice permeated the clinical atmosphere. Leonie instantly let go of Scott's hand and searched her pockets for a handkerchief. She had been so absorbed in trying to reach Scott that she hadn't heard the door opening or the visitor arriving.

"Miss Scot. I didn't know you were here. I heard you'd left the district."

Penny Scot strode to the far side of the bed carrying a bunch of flowers which she deposited clumsily on the side trolley. She hardly looked in Scott's direction.

"I have been away for while. Scott and I thought it was for the best. We needed time to sort out our true feelings for each other. I returned for Christmas and heard about the accident. I came immediately to give Mrs Andrews some moral support."

Leonie got up. She didn't wish to hear any more. "How very thoughtful,

I'm sure Mrs Andrews appreciates it. She will be back in a minute. I only came because Scott was asking for me."

"I don't know what good you think you were doing. He can't hear you. We've all been trying to communicate with him without success. Goodness knows why he called your name except possibly to revile you. We thought we'd got rid of you for good. Scott said he never wanted to see you again."

"I must go." Leonie gathered together her belongings and with a last look at Scott stumbled from the room. Tears stung her eyes. She almost bumped into Mrs Andrews in the doorway and mumbled an apology.

"Thank you for coming," his mother said. "I hope you didn't mind."

"Not at all," Leonie replied. "I'm only sorry that there is nothing I can do."

She would have hurried away but Mrs Andrews caught hold of her sleeve. "Jane told me that you were business associates so I thought, since business is all Scott ever thinks about that you might just do the trick. Thank you for trying, I do appreciate it. You take care of yourself now and drive carefully. I do believe snow is forecast. I hope you haven't far to go."

How Leonie got safely back to the cottage she would never know. She had never been so unhappy, her thoughts see-sawing intolerably. The sight of Scott looking so helpless and impotent had been horrifying. He always looked so much larger than life and more than capable of taking care of himself. She only hoped that his injuries were not as bad as they appeared and that he pulled through before long. If that happened she knew that she would have to see him — just once more. She would have to find out how much he heard of her confession — maybe none of it in which case she was unsure of how to proceed.

She rang Tina who was in constant touch with Jane and Andrews Electronics and gave her Mrs Cherry's phone number. She asked her to ring if she heard anything — any news at all about Scott. She was beginning to regret having talked so much. She wasn't sure just how much of the dialogue Penny had overheard or how much Scott might have taken in either. Maybe nothing at all and if so it had been a wasted journey and possibly given Penny more ammunition to use against her.

The next day Mrs Cherry called round with good news — Scott was out of the coma. The doctors were satisfied with his progress and forecasting that he would make a full recovery but it would take time. Leonie breathed a sigh of relief. That was a start. What happened next was going to be up to Scott.

She was in the middle of wrapping up presents to take with her to the Chandlers and when Mrs Cherry left Leonie walked across to give Bruno a hug. The bear was such a comfort to her still, he was the one thing she would never ever part with.

Suddenly she made up her mind and throwing on a coat she snatched up her bag and hurried out to her car. She drove the four miles to town pleased that there was something positive she could do which she hoped would precipitate a response from Scott.

She went in search of a toy shop. It took her a little while to find somewhere to park and then had a tussle fighting her way through the crowds of Christmas shoppers in the town centre. Eventually she located a large store which boasted a toy department complete with Santa's Grotto. There she bought a huge teddy bear — the largest they had in stock, one not unlike her own.

The assistant, when Leonie mentioned the hospital, obligingly agreed to parcel it up and send it express delivery for her. Leonie returned home smiling wistfully. At least Penny wouldn't know who had sent the bear, but Scott would.

10

LEONIE arrived at the Chandlers as arranged three days before Christmas. At the last minute she had doubts about going, but Mrs Cherry was most persuasive. If Leonie wasn't going away for the holiday then she declared that she would have to stay at home too. She didn't think it wise for Leonie to be there all alone in her condition, even though Leonie protested that the baby wasn't due for several more weeks. Leonie gave in, she couldn't have Mrs Cherry missing out on the opportunity of seeing her own grandchildren, especially on such a festive occasion.

Leonie wasn't feeling very festive though and didn't want her gloom to spoil anyone else's Christmas. She was depressed because she hadn't had any come-back from her get well present.

She wasn't sure what she had expected or rather hoped for. At any rate Scott hadn't rushed to offer to marry her. She heard that he'd been released from hospital, but according to Tina very much against medical advice.

When Leonie arrived at the Chandlers Cynthia greeted her like a long lost friend. "It is good to see you, Leonie. The boys have asked me almost every day for the past week when you were coming. I hope you've got a full repertoire of stories to tell them."

"It's good of you to have me, especially looking like this." Leonie patted her tummy.

"Lively is he?" Cynthia asked with a knowing grin.

"Going to be a footballer I surmise."

"You've been keeping well I gather. Still determined to go through with the adoption?"

"Yes, I guess I am. I don't have much choice really. How are Gerry and the boys?" she asked not wanting to dwell on that particular topic of conversation. As the time drew ever nearer she was becoming more and more possessive and knew it was going to be the hardest thing she had ever had to do in her life. She had thought and thought of feasible alternatives but it was no use. She knew from her own experience that she had to have the baby adopted at birth for it to have the best chance in life.

"They're fine. Gerry is in his study, but should be out soon. He's putting the final touches to one of his books, but promised me faithfully that he would help with the decorations. I haven't even made a start on the baking yet, never mind the decorating of the Christmas tree. He's going to be barred from the study until after New Year no matter what his publisher thinks. The boys will be home from school soon. They are as excited as a wagon load of monkeys, and can't wait for Christmas to come. Unpack your things and I'll go and put the kettle on. I'm sure you must be ready for a cuppa. We'll have it in the kitchen where it's nice and warm and you can tell me all your news."

Leonie sat on the bed for a moment savouring the friendly way that Cynthia had made her feel at home. This is what it should be like. This was a family home, and she was determined that her child would have one too. A proper mother and father who would love and care for it, and provide a happy lifestyle. She wished with all her heart that she could be that mother, but it would appear that it was not to be. Oh, Scott why didn't you ring?

* * *

Christmas was wonderful. Leonie thoroughly enjoyed it, despite her earlier reservations. The Chandler family made her feel so welcome. It reminded her of when she was little, joining in with the preparations — the trimmings — the Christmas tree — the carol service and the happy togetherness. She did momentarily wonder what she would be doing in a year's time, but managed to successfully blank it out reasonably well. First things first she reflected. A lot could happen in a year as she knew only too well.

She was going to return to the cottage the day after Boxing day but Cynthia and Gerry both badgered her to stay on until after New Year and since she had no reason to return any sooner she accepted gratefully. She wasn't looking forward to being on her own again especially as Mrs Cherry would still be away.

"I have an appointment on the third of January though for a check up," she said, "I must be back for that."

"That's great. You won't have to travel back on New Year's Day. We've invited a few friends round to let the New Year in so we like the next day to recover. Last year it got a bit exhausting and it was four o'clock in the morning when the last one left," Gerry grumbled with a shake of the head.

"Oh, in that case . . . "

"You're to stay," Cynthia said. "You can always go up to your room at any time you feel like it, but I think you'll enjoy yourself. We've only invited a few of the neighbours, and some friends and relatives that we didn't see over Christmas. It's nice occasionally to have a get together and we never seem to get round to it during the rest of the year for some reason or another. This year it's our way of thanking them for their kindness when I was ill. Gerry was well looked after by one and all. In fact I do believe he put on weight while I was in hospital, he was so well fed."

Leonie rang Tina to wish her a happy New Year and learned that Scott was not only out of hospital but indeed back at work — at least for a short time each day. They couldn't keep him away. Jane said his family was extremely concerned but there was nothing they could do about it. He was being his usual pig-headed self and nothing anyone said did any good. They were just keeping their fingers crossed that he didn't have a relapse.

Leonie recounted all to Cynthia who listened sympathetically. "He must be tough," she remarked. "Either that or plain stupid. Maybe . . . No, forget I said that. You have to play the hand as it's dealt. I expect he's doing what he feels he must do, just like you are."

"I will go and see him — in the New Year," Leonie said. "When I visited him in hospital I promised I would talk to him before having the baby adopted. I don't know how much he heard mind you."

"Good," was all Cynthia said.

* * *

New Year's Eve arrived. Leonie didn't feel too bright, she'd had a poor night. She wasn't looking forward to the party and wished she hadn't agreed to stay. She probably wouldn't know anyone and knew she would feel out of place in her condition.

After breakfast Gerry set off with the boys. He was taking them to stay with Cynthia's sister overnight.

"It's as well that he's out of the way," grinned Cynthia as she waved them off. "We can do without him under our feet when there's work to be done."

Cynthia and Leonie spent the whole day preparing for the party. It was going to be a buffet supper but it took them most of the day organising the rooms to provide more space for extra seating and arranging the table which groaned under the weight of Cynthia's party fare.

"I thought you said a few friends were coming!" laughed Leonie as she tried to squeeze another plate of vol au vents on to the already overflowing table. "You've enough here to feed an army."

"I wouldn't want to run short of anything," Cynthia said solemnly counting the glasses. "And I told them all they could bring anyone else along with them so I don't know how many I'm catering for. I think we're about ready don't you, so why don't you go and run your bath while I finish off." She looked at the clock on the mantel piece. "You'll have time to put your feet up for an hour before the first guests arrive. I hope Gerry won't be late. I wonder where he's got to? I thought he'd have been back by now."

* * *

Leonie wished that she had brought another dress with her. She hadn't many outfits she could still get into, but settled for the one she'd worn at Christmas, conscious that it wouldn't really matter anyway. She probably wouldn't spend long among the guests — just long enough to greet the Chandler's friends and then she intended retiring early. She wasn't feeling in a party mood, her extra weight was definitely off-putting.

It wasn't only that which was depressing her though. Soon she would have to make contact with Scott. She had promised she would and Cynthia would see to it that she kept her promise so she couldn't back out even if she wanted to. She heard Gerry return and a lot of chatter down in the kitchen. She hoped there hadn't been a problem with the children. Gerry had been much later than Cynthia had expected. However they both appeared quite happy when she went downstairs.

Once the party began and Leonie had met most of the guests she made herself useful in the kitchen washing up glasses and replenishing plates as the eats were demolished. She knew Cynthia wanted her to meet everybody and hazarded a guess as to why. She felt sure that two of them had an ulterior motive for being there — the couple who wanted to adopt a child. She thought she had identified them but of course said nothing; she might have guessed wrong.

Cynthia told her in passing that there was still another guest expected whom she particularly wanted her to meet. She didn't say who so Leonie dutifully returned to the sitting room and fended off the endless questions about the baby she was so obviously expecting. Everyone was most considerate, and kept offering her advice, but since most of them didn't realise she wasn't going to keep the baby she felt like screaming.

By nine-thirty she began to wilt. She wondered if she had been standing for too long so retreated into the kitchen for a glass of water. She felt decidedly odd but didn't wish to cause a commotion amongst the guests, so she sat down on a stool sipping the water, hoping that she would soon recover. Maybe it's the heat she thought, she was perspiring quite freely. With so many people milling about they didn't really need the coal fire, and the stuffy atmosphere was a little overpowering.

Deciding that she would have to call it a day and she was about to go and find Cynthia to tell her that she was going up to her room, when a young man sauntered in with an empty wine bottle. She remembered his name was Derek or was it Darrel? She vaguely remembered him arriving with his wife — a petite dark haired young woman. Leonie tried to think of something suitable to say but her head felt all woozy, and she had strange sinking feeling.

"I say, are you all right?"

She nodded groggily. "Fine. It's just so hot."

He grinned. "Sure is. Can I get you some ice for your drink?"

The front door bell chimed and Leonie saw Cynthia hurrying to answer it. The last guest had arrived.

It couldn't be! That voice! She must be hearing things. What was *he* doing here? The next minute there was a clatter as the young man dropped the ice cube tray in the sink and hurried to Leonie's side arriving just in time to catch her as she slithered from the stool. Dimly she heard him call out for assistance before complete oblivion overcame her.

The next few hours were a blur. Leonie vaguely remembered hushed voices and the sound of an ambulance. She kept apologising to everyone for spoiling their party. It seemed like an endless journey with the siren ringing insistently and Cynthia's voice encouragingly calm, but all Leonie saw was Scott. She wondered if she had been hallucinating. Had she really seen him kissing Cynthia under the mistletoe? It couldn't have been him surely and yet —

* * *

Leonie eventually woke to find Scott's sleepy eyes watching her. He looked tired and worried, but smiled wanly when he saw her open her eyes.

"You know you shouldn't eat garlic,"

he teased. "I thought you knew better than that. How are you feeling, sweetheart?"

"Scott? What . . . where . . . ?" Had he really called her sweetheart?

"Hush, love. All in good time. Why is it that every time we meet up you are in another man's arms?"

There he goes again she thought, getting the wrong impression.

"I don't know. I'm confused. How come you are here?" Biting back tears she asked, "The baby? I was going to . . . "

"We have a beautiful, bouncing baby daughter. She's going to have the most glorious mop of honey gold hair according to the doctor. The nurse has taken her away for the moment but they said they'd bring her back when you woke up. She's a shade underweight but they assure me that she's fine."

"I don't want to see her." The tears came thick and fast now. She rolled over so that she couldn't see him. "I can't . . . "

"Leonie, look at me. You don't really mean that. Not now — now that I know the truth. You should have told me what was going on. I've been out of my mind these last few months," he reprimanded her gently, bending over to kiss her.

"If I'd told you, you would have blamed me for being devious," she said turning over and trying to sit up. "Besides, you and Penny . . . "

"Later, honey." He assisted her to a comfortable position and then sat on the edge of the bed so that he could put an arm around her. "I'll explain everything later. For the moment you have to get your strength back. Cynthia told me how you felt and all I can say is that I'm very, very sorry to have put you through so much misery, but I'll make it up to you, I promise. I know how much being part of a family must mean to you."

"Oh, Scott," she sighed and put her head on his shoulder. "I felt certain it was going to be a boy and he'd look exactly like you."

"Maybe the next one, huh?" Gently he bent to kiss away her tears and laughed gently. "You do make a habit of being found in compromising situations don't you?"

"No I don't. You misread everything I do."

"Well, we won't argue about it now."

"Are you all right?" she asked scanning his face for signs of his injuries. "You looked terrible when I came to see you in hospital."

"I'm fine. Once a certain bear turned up at my bedside and I knew I hadn't been dreaming I couldn't get out of there quick enough."

She reached up to touch one of the bruises he sported. They were fading but still visible. "Why didn't you contact me sooner then?" she asked softly.

Kissing the inside of her hand he murmured. "Maybe if you'd left me a clue of your whereabouts it would have helped."

"Tina knew."

"I guessed as much but Tina wasn't home. I called several times once I got out of hospital but she was never there. No-one could tell me where to find you. It was if you'd been spirited away into thin air again."

"I forgot, she was spending Christmas and New Year with her in-laws. So how did you find me?"

"I tried everyone I could think of but drew a blank every time. I've made mother's life intolerable complaining that she should have found out where you were staying when she had the chance. I even discovered where you bought the bear but that was another dead end since you paid with cash. I've had a most miserable Christmas going quietly berserk.

"Bumping into Gerry today, or rather yesterday was an incredible piece of luck."

"You met Gerry? Where?"

"In Chellow would you believe. I've haunted Chellow since you left. Every spare moment of my time I've tramped the streets hoping that I'd find some lead to your whereabouts. Then low and behold I was coming out of the bookshop near where your shop used to be and I thought I recognised the man just entering. He looked different with his clothes on but something clicked into place."

"Good heavens. And Gerry told you where I was?"

"Not straight away he wouldn't. I had the devil's own job convincing him that I desperately needed to see you and that I was truly concerned about you."

"I wonder what Gerry was doing in Chellow. He was supposed to be at his sister-in-law's. You know I wouldn't be at all surprised if Cynthia put him up to it."

Scott nodded in agreement. "That's what I've been sitting here wondering. He told me at the time that he liked to visit the bookshops in the locality to see how well his books were displayed but I got the impression it was just an excuse. He looked rather uncomfortable, but I thought at the time it was because he disliked me and I couldn't say I'd blame him after the scene on the beach. Leonie, my love. You will marry me now won't you? I can't promise you great wealth or a fine house even . . . "

"Scott, before you say any more. How much do you remember — if any — of what I told you when I visited you in hospital? I want you to know everything before you commit yourself."

"I know that I love you and that is sufficient for me. Do you honestly believe I care a jot about what scandal the press came up with? I wish I had met your parents, and I'm sure they would be justifiably proud of their beautiful daughter, and all that she has achieved.

"After I returned from Spain I dragged it out of Penny exactly what she had been up to. She said she was trying to protect me from making a fool of myself. She said she believed what the reporters wrote — Dean showed her a copy of the newspaper.

"It was Penny who sent out those letters, signing my signature, which she does better than me I might add. She also confessed that she opened the letter which you left at my flat and burned it. She used to pop in to see that everything was in order while I was away because I was in the process of selling it remember."

"She led me to believe that you were there with her at the time. She was wearing your dressing gown and she intimated that you and she . . ."

"There was never anything like that between us, Leonie, my love. When I was abroad she sometimes stayed overnight at my flat. She said it was more convenient because of the longer hours she was putting in and my flat was closer to work. In the circumstances I could hardly object."

"So what happened? Tina told me

that you'd had a row and that you were running the show now."

"I managed to sell the flat and I moved back in with mother like I told you I was going to. I hope you won't mind sharing my bachelor pad for a while until I can make other arrangements?"

"You seem to have taken it for granted what my answer is," she said cheekily.

"I'm taking no chances this time. I may not be able to buy you all the expensive clothes you're used to — not yet any way, but I promise I'll make it up to you soon. We'll make a great team you and I. I'll try to find someone to do some of the trips abroad — at least until young madam is able to be either left or taken with us. Whichever you think will be most appropriate."

"Scott. I have another confession to make. My clothes cost very little — they come from a nearly new shop. I did the accounts for the owner and she used to keep items aside which she thought would appeal to me. I don't cost a fortune to keep."

"I might have known I suppose. I misjudged you about everything else. My darling, sweet Leonie can you find it in your heart to forgive me?" He deposited light butterfly kisses on her neck, ran his hands through her hair and she sighed with satisfaction. "I was told not to overtire you," he murmured, "you had a difficult time. I should go and give mother the best news she's had in years. It will make up for the horrible time I gave her over Christmas."

As Scott got up to go Leonie settled back against the pillows with a wistful sigh. "I liked your mother, Scott. I hope she won't be too disappointed with me."

"Not a chance. She's going to be over the moon to have you for a daughter-in-law, especially complete with granddaughter. She was worried about you actually. Jane told her you were a business acquaintance so she was surprised to see you were pregnant. If she had known she wouldn't have asked you to drive to the hospital to see me I guess, in view of the weather."

"I'm glad she did. She was frightfully worried about you and I was afraid you were going to die before I had a chance to tell you how very much I love you."

"Oh, Leonie, I do love you so. Normally I would have despatched the thugs quite easily, but I'd had the stuffing knocked out of me during the preceding few months. They came at me wielding batons and floored me before I had a chance to defend myself. The next thing I remember was an angel telling me that I was going to be a father, and that I couldn't die because she needed me. I thought it might have been an illusion, but when I received the get well present I knew that it had been no dream."

"I couldn't think of what else to do after . . . after what Penny said. I didn't know if you did still want me."

"I take it that means you will marry me."

"Yes, if you'll have me, Scott. Your daughter needs a father and I need you."

"Sleep now, my darling. I'll be back soon. Oh, and by the way I think you ought to have these back." He handed her the tear-drop earrings. "They don't suit me anyway."

11

"SO you are the one who has had my son all at sixes and sevens." Mrs Andrews arrived at visiting time with a huge bouquet of flowers. "I'm delighted to meet you again, Leonie. Scott has told me everything and you are not to worry. You'll have to forgive an old woman for being slightly sentimental at a time like this. I can't tell you how happy I am to have you join our family."

"Hello, Mrs Andrews. It is nice to see you again too. Thank you for the flowers, they are beautiful."

Leonie had been apprehensive about meeting her mother-in-law to be, despite Scott's claim that she would be delighted.

"She's come to see the memento from Austria," Scott whispered as he bent to kiss her.

Leonie giggled. "Would you care to take the baby for a moment, Mrs Andrews?"

"Oh, may I?" she said.

Scott's eyes darkened as he winked at Leonie, appreciating her thoughtfulness.

"She's got your eyes, Scott. Look. She's beautiful, just like you, my dear. My first grandchild. What a wonderful way to begin the New Year."

"How are you feeling, sweetheart? Mother has all sorts of plans already on the drawing board. I hope you feel up to it? She's mentally preparing the nursery for your homecoming, and if I'm not mistaken planning to raid the baby care department of Brad's the moment it opens."

"I hope you'll let Scott bring you back to stay with us," his mother urged. "It will be lovely to have the nursery in use again."

"It appears my apartment is not suitable?" Scott murmured.

"Of course it isn't," his mother said. "Leonie must have time to get accustomed to everyone before she decides how best to proceed. Don't let him bully you, my dear. I don't suppose you had anything organised since I gather it was rather premature. But not to worry, we'll take care of you."

"Thank you," Leonie said smiling her gratitude. "Everything is happening so quickly." She looked up at Scott for comment about his mother's suggestion but he seemed more interested in examining his daughter.

Mrs Andrews saw the interchange and handed the baby to her son. "I must go and leave you to make your plans. I don't want to be accused of being an interfering mother-in-law already. I just had to come and offer you my congratulations, dear."

* * *

Once his mother left Scott went to sit on the bed next to Leonie. She looked at the gentle way he held his daughter and felt a tear of affection run down her cheek. It made a wonderful picture.

"Would you mind staying with mother for a while?"

Leonie grinned, his mother might only be small but she was a force to be reckoned with. She had Scott exactly where she wanted him. For the moment though the she was happy to go along with their suggestions.

"I think it is extremely kind of her. I must admit that I'm nervous about coping with the baby on my own. I wasn't going to . . . "

"I'll do my share, but it looks as if I'm banned to my apartment until we get married. Mother has this quaint idea that we should have a proper wedding and I am to behave with restraint until our wedding night. You won't keep me waiting long will you?"

She smiled at his pained look.

"Scott. Please would you clarify something for me. Why was Penny so vindictive towards me? Did she really want to marry you after all? Was she in love with you?"

Placing the baby back in its crib Scott returned to sit by Leonie. "It goes back over a year. Penny ran a shop — a clothes shop of some sort, women's fashions I believe. Anyway, it got into difficulties and had to close down. She probably lost a bundle. Whether by her own mis-management or not I've no idea.

"She couldn't find another job locally so she began working for us in the office. It was supposed to be a temporary measure to tide her over until she found something suitable. Then as you know her brother was killed. She used to share a flat with Andy and apparently she couldn't keep up the repayments on the mortgage without her brother's share — they paid fifty-fifty."

"So she set her cap at you."

"Sort of. She cunningly set Dean and me off against each other. Dean wanted a slice of Andrews Electronics and Penny wanted to start another business. Dean offered to finance her if she sold him Andy's shares. Fortunately Penny didn't realise that she could have done so. She thought she had to give me first refusal.

"I believe somewhere along the line Penny expected to marry Dean but when she learned he had no such intention she thought she may as well latch on to me. Without Andy she seemed lost and needed someone, and I happened to be her choicc. She had got herself into a financial muddle and was looking for an easy way out. She told Dean that you were causing problems, that we were having an affair and it could ruin everything.

"I suppose when she read the letter you left telling me that you suspected that you were pregnant she became seriously worried. She had to find a way of discrediting you. She already knew Dean held the lease for your property so she told him not to renew it and then she contacted all the local businesses she could, telling them that you weren't to be trusted."

"To put me out of business."

"Of course. She was jealous of your success. You had managed to build up a flourishing business which galled her intensely. Not only that but you had men falling over themselves to help you and sing your praises — Dean in particular.

"She knew all too well the reaction of the people of Chellow once scandal spread about you though. I'm sorry, Leonie. It was all my doing, by trying to protect my own business. I was too wrapped up in my own affairs to notice what was going on."

"I don't blame you, Scott. I don't blame Simon either. He did me a favour. He could have simply refused to renew the lease but he didn't. He made me a good deal — sufficient for me to leave the district straightaway."

"I'm not sure if I can agree with your summing up, but can we forget the pair of them now? I've had it up to here with their wheeling and dealing. The last I heard Penny has sold the flat and is back in London. Dean, I suspect will be a thorn in our sides from time to time but something we shall have to put up with."

* * *

Three months later Leonie and Scott shook the remains of the confetti from their hair and clothes as they waited for their flight.

"It seems a long way to go for a few days," she whispered. "I wish we could be spirited there in minutes. Maybe we should have gone to the Lake District after all."

"I know what you mean," he grinned. "You must admit I've been a model fiancé, but now that I am your husband I am eager to indulge in some husbandly privileges."

"Has it been so hard," she teased.

"Want to feel," he murmured making her blush. "It's been nearly a year dammit. Just you wait until we get to our hotel. We shan't stir from our room even to eat."

"Why, Mr Andrews! And I thought you were taking me to Austria to learn to ski!"

"Not this trip, I'm not," he growled.

"I hope Jolene is all right."

"I know you miss her, honey. So do I, but a honeymoon is no place for a baby."

"Your mother was delighted to be entrusted with her wasn't she? You know Scott I've been thinking."

"Now why should that make me nervous?"

She mockingly punched him in the chest. "I miss being involved in business activities, and I . . . well, this may strike you as totally impractical, but do you think I could participate more in your work."

"What had you in mind?"

"Well, with your mother more than pleased to look after Jolene, I could take over some of the office paper work and perhaps accompany you on sales trips."

His eyes flashed. "You mean you are happy to leave Jolene behind? I was afraid to suggest it knowing how you feel about family togetherness."

"We wouldn't leave her for long, and she would be well cared for by an adoring grandmother and thoroughly spoilt by her aunt. I can't tell you how much I appreciate the warm welcome your family has given me. When I think about what I would have missed if . . . Anyway, I always wanted to see something of the world, and I don't like the idea of you spending long, lonely nights away from home in some exotic place unsupervised. You're far too handsome to be allowed such lassitude."

"If you remember I did suggest something along those lines before."

* * *

It was late evening when they arrived at their hotel in Inton — the same one they had stayed on the previous visit. This time though they had a marvellous double room with doors leading out onto the balcony. Leonie stood by the window gazing out at the snow capped mountains thinking about the past year. Scott crept up behind her and pulled her back into his arms.

"How about that tango you promised me so long ago?"

She chuckled. "I'm afraid to admit that I can't dance."

"You can dance the tango I have in mind, I promise you." Turning her around he hugged her gently and kissed the tip of her nose. "Happy, sweetheart? Alone at last."

"Yes," she whispered "but would you believe I'm a little bit shy. I know it's our honeymoon and it's not the first time . . . but I . . . "

"Shall I tell you something, my darling wife? You're not the only one who's nervous. I'm scared out of my wits wondering if I can perform satisfactorily for you. You are up there on your pedestal, looking incredibly beautiful having produced a divine daughter almost completely by yourself. I don't feel I deserve such a wonderful, clever wife. I only hope that you will be gentle with me since I am a little out of practice. I seem to remember you were extremely intoxicating when aroused — in fact a right little raver."

Slowly he began to undo the buttons of her blouse and she tentatively followed suit but he caught hold of her hands.

"I want this to be the most perfect lovemaking I can make it. If you touch me all will be lost." His eyes travelled down with a wry grin. "Allow me just this once to show you that I am not the callow youth I demonstrated in the past. This time let us take it slowly so that I can sensitise every nerve end you possess. This time I want to make love with you not simply to have unbridled sex."

He proceeded to undress her while she stood hypnotised by the erotic feelings he was already arousing. She didn't know how long she could refrain from touching him. She longed to hold him, to slide her hands over his broad shoulders and to nuzzle against his impressive chest, but the torture he was inflicting was mind blowing.

"Motherhood suits you," he whispered scooping her into his arms and transferring her to the bed. "You are even more beautiful than I remembered."

He gazed down at her lying naked on top of the duvet while quickly shedding his own clothes.

She wasn't at all embarrassed now. She was drunk with power. She had this wonderful, virile man to have and to hold until death parted them, which she was going to make certain was a long, long way off.

His kisses wound their magic and his roving hands massaged, coaxed and caressed. Together they recaptured the electrifying feeling that enshrined them both. Each seemingly aware of what pleased the other and happy to provide as necessary so that they gained maximum enjoyment.

"If this is what you are like when you are shy, heaven help us when you overcome it," he teased. He had held back as long as he could, but with a cry of fulfilment he took them both to even greater heights than they'd hitherto reached.

"Now tell me you can't tango!" he chuckled as they lay totally spent in each other's arms.

Leonie's last thought before she fell into a deep, satisfying sleep was to thank Jolie for sending her the most wonderful husband in the whole world.

THE END

Other titles in the Linford Romance Library:

A YOUNG MAN'S FANCY
Nancy Bell

Six people get together for reasons of their own, and the result is one of misunderstanding, suspicion and mounting tension.

THE WISDOM OF LOVE
Janey Blair

Barbie meets Louis and receives flattering proposals, but her reawakened affection for Jonah develops into an overwhelming passion.

MIRAGE IN THE MOONLIGHT
Mandy Brown

En route to an island to be secretary to a multi-millionaire, Heather's stubborn loyalty to her former flatmate plunges her into a grim hazard.

WITH SOMEBODY ELSE
Theresa Charles

Rosamond sets off for Cornwall with Hugo to meet his family, blissfully unaware of the shocks in store for her.

A SUMMER FOR STRANGERS
Claire Hamilton

Because she had lost her job, her flat and she had no money, Tabitha agreed to pose as Adam's future wife although she believed the scheme to be deceitful and cruel.

VILLA OF SINGING WATER
Angela Petron

The disquieting incidents that occurred at the Vatican and the Colosseum did not trouble Jan at first, but then they became increasingly unpleasant and alarming.

DOCTOR NAPIER'S NURSE
Pauline Ash

When cousins Midge and Derry are entered as probationer nurses on the same day but at different hospitals they agree to exchange identities.

A GIRL LIKE JULIE
Louise Ellis

Caroline absolutely adored Hugh Barrington, but then Julie Crane came into their lives. Julie was the kind of girl who attracts men without even trying.

COUNTRY DOCTOR
Paula Lindsay

When Evan Richmond bought a practice in a remote country village he did not realise that a casual encounter would lead to the loss of his heart.

ENCORE
Helga Moray

Craig and Janet realise that their true happiness lies with each other, but it is only under traumatic circumstances that they can be reunited.

NICOLETTE
Ivy Preston

When Grant Alston came back into her life, Nicolette was faced with a dilemma. Should she follow the path of duty or the path of love?

THE GOLDEN PUMA
Margaret Way

Catherine's time was spent looking after her father's Queensland farm. But what life was there without David, who wasn't interested in her?

HOSPITAL BY THE LAKE
Anne Durham

Nurse Marguerite Ingleby was always ready to become personally involved with her patients, to the despair of Brian Field, the Senior Surgical Registrar, who loved her.

VALLEY OF CONFLICT
David Farrell

Isolated in a hostel in the French Alps, Ann Russell sees her fiancé being seduced by a young girl. Then comes the avalanche that imperils their lives.

NURSE'S CHOICE
Peggy Gaddis

A proposal of marriage from the incredibly handsome and wealthy Reagan was enough to upset any girl — and Brooke Martin was no exception.

A DANGEROUS MAN
Anne Goring

Photographer Polly Burton was on safari in Mombasa when she met enigmatic Leon Hammond. But unpredictability was the name of the game where Leon was concerned.

PRECIOUS INHERITANCE
Joan Moules

Karen's new life working for an authoress took her from Sussex to a foreign airstrip and a kidnapping; to a real life adventure as gripping as any in the books she typed.

VISION OF LOVE
Grace Richmond

When Kathy takes over the rundown country kennels she finds Alec Stinton, a local vet, very helpful. But their friendship arouses bitter jealousy and a tragedy seems inevitable.

CRUSADING NURSE
Jane Converse

It was handsome Dr. Corbett who opened Nurse Susan Leighton's eyes and who set her off on a lonely crusade against some powerful enemies and a shattering struggle against the man she loved.

WILD ENCHANTMENT
Christina Green

Rowan's agreeable new boss had a dream of creating a famous perfume using her precious Silverstar, but Rowan's plans were very different.

DESERT ROMANCE
Irene Ord

Sally agrees to take her sister Pam's place as La Chartreuse the dancer, but she finds out there is more to it than dyeing her hair red and looking like her sister.

HEART OF ICE
Marie Sidney

How was January to know that not only would the warmth of the Swiss people thaw out her frozen heart, but that she too would play her part in helping someone to live again?

LUCKY IN LOVE
Margaret Wood

Companion-secretary to wealthy gambler Laura Duxford, who lived in Monaco, seemed to Melanie a fabulous job. Especially as Melanie had already lost her heart to Laura's son, Julian.

NURSE TO PRINCESS JASMINE
Lilian Woodward

Nick's surgeon brother, Tom, performs an operation on an Arabian princess, and she invites Tom, Nick and his fiancé to Omander, where a web of deceit and intrigue closes about them.